12/14

STONE ARCH BOOKS
a capstone imprint

▼▼ STONE ARCH BOOKS™

Published in 2014 by Stone Arch Books
A Capstone Imprint
1710 Roe Crest Drive
North Mankato, MN 56003
www.capstonepub.com

Originally published by DC Comics in the U.S. in single
magazine form as Batman: Li'l Gotham.
Copyright © 2014 DC Comics. All Rights Reserved.

DC Comics
1700 Broadway, New York, NY 10019
A Warner Bros. Entertainment Company
No part of this publication may be reproduced in
whole or in part, or stored in a retrieval system,
or transmitted in any form or by any means,
electronic, mechanical, photocopying, recording, or
otherwise, without written permission.

Printed in China.
032014   008085LEOF14

Cataloging-in-Publication Data is available at the
Library of Congress website:
ISBN: 978-1-4342-9218-6 (library binding)

Summary: On Valentine's Day, Joker's plans to
become Cupid backfire when all of Gotham's women
relentlessly pursue him. Will Batman be able to
save the Joker from the not-so-angry mob - not
to mention Harley Quinn's wrath? Then, during the
Lunar New Year's celebration in Chinatown, a rare
artifact is stolen. Damian Wayne, Bruce's son, takes
the case. Along the way, he gets a history lesson
from Alfred in addition to a real mean martial arts
lesson from Katana!

STONE ARCH BOOKS
Ashley C. Andersen Zantop Publisher
Michael Dahl Editorial Director
Sean Tulien Editor
Heather Kindseth Creative Director
Bob Lentz Art Director
Hilary Wacholz Designer
Kathy McColley Production Specialist

DC Comics
Sarah Gaydos Original U.S. Editor

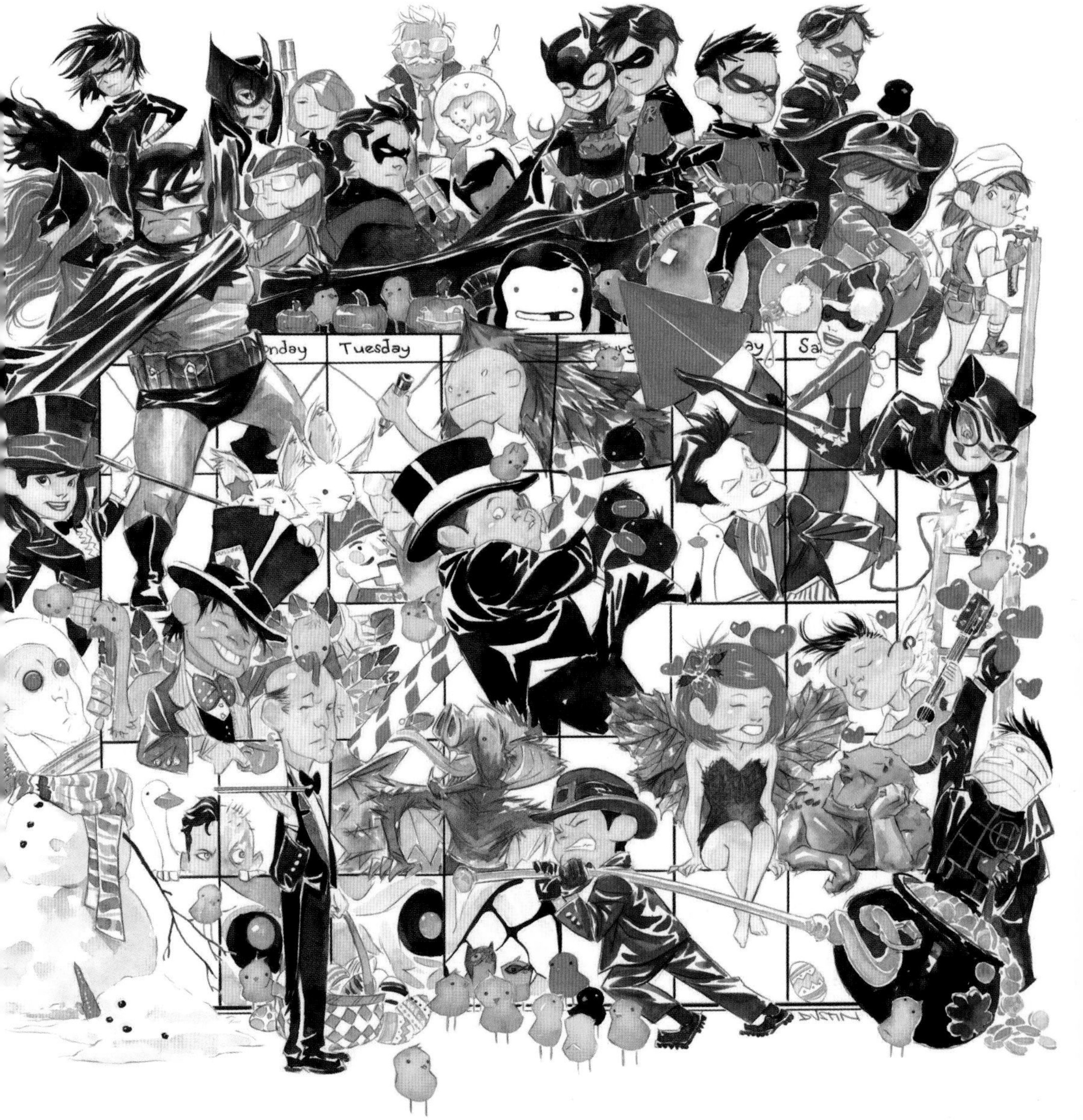
Tuesday
DUSTIN

VALENTINE'S DAY AND THE LUNAR NEW YEAR

Dustin Nguyen & Derek Fridolfs....................... writers
Dustin Nguyen.. artist
Saida Temofonte..letterer

BATMAN created by
Bob Kane

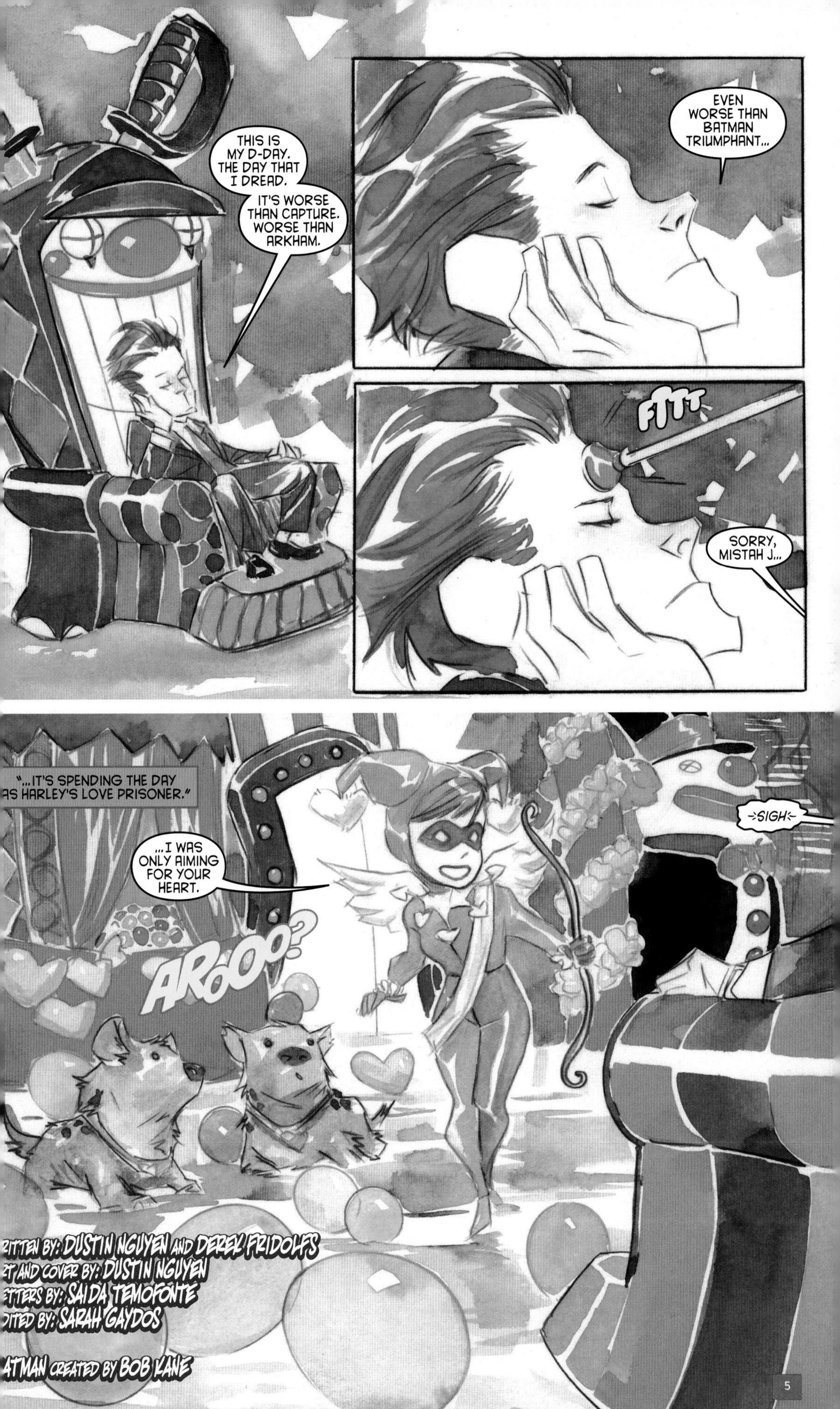

THIS IS MY D-DAY. THE DAY THAT I DREAD.
IT'S WORSE THAN CAPTURE. WORSE THAN ARKHAM.
EVEN WORSE THAN BATMAN TRIUMPHANT...
FTTT
SORRY, MISTAH J...
"...IT'S SPENDING THE DAY AS HARLEY'S LOVE PRISONER."
...I WAS ONLY AIMING FOR YOUR HEART.
-SIGH-
AROOO?
RITTEN BY: DUSTIN NGUYEN AND DEREK FRIDOLFS
RT AND COVER BY: DUSTIN NGUYEN
ETTERS BY: SAIDA TEMOFONTE
DITED BY: SARAH GAYDOS
ATMAN CREATED BY BOB KANE

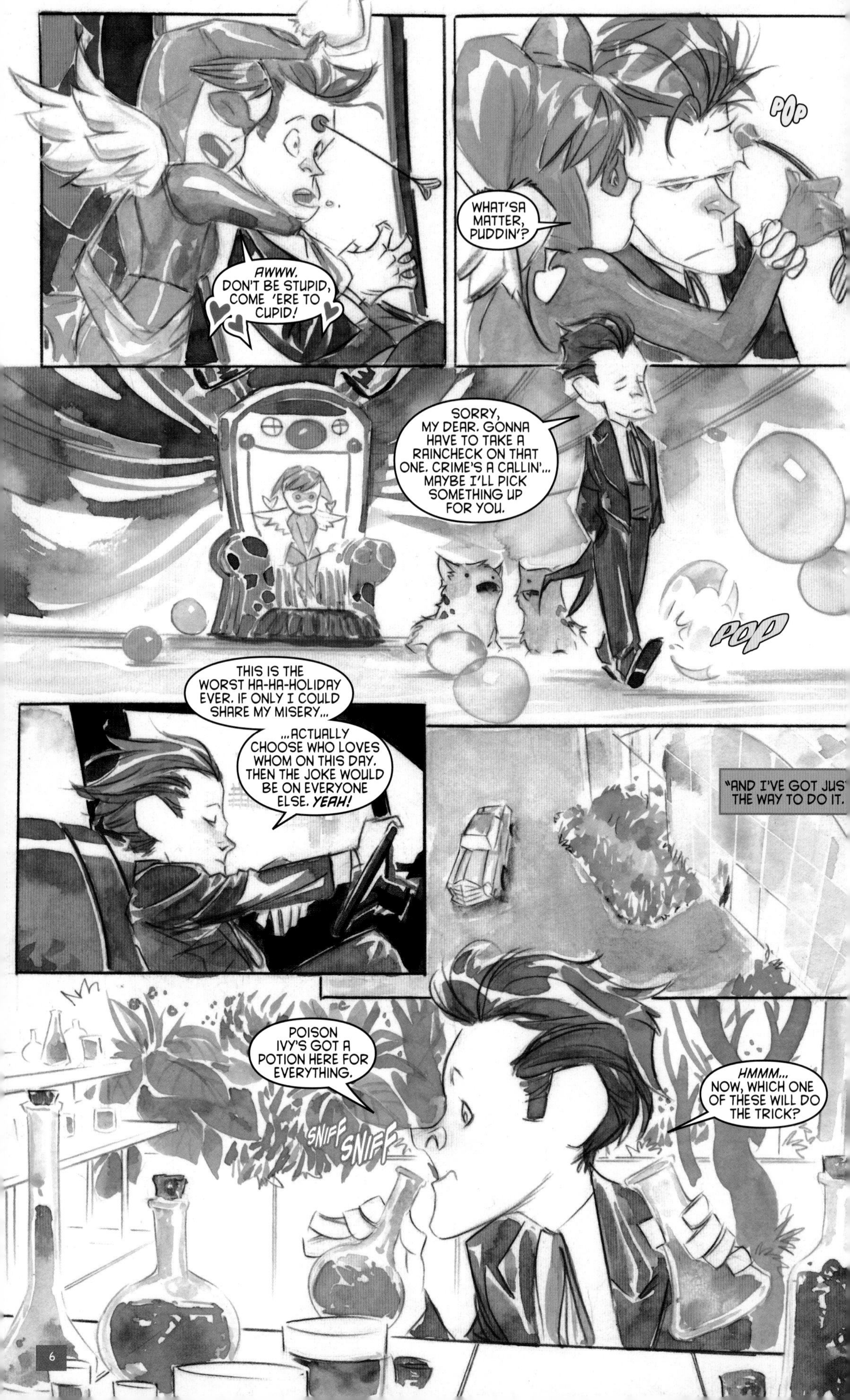
AWWW. DON'T BE STUPID, COME 'ERE TO CUPID!
WHAT'SA MATTER, PUDDIN'?
POP
SORRY, MY DEAR. GONNA HAVE TO TAKE A RAINCHECK ON THAT ONE. CRIME'S A CALLIN'... MAYBE I'LL PICK SOMETHING UP FOR YOU.
POP
THIS IS THE WORST HA-HA-HOLIDAY EVER. IF ONLY I COULD SHARE MY MISERY...
...ACTUALLY CHOOSE WHO LOVES WHOM ON THIS DAY. THEN THE JOKE WOULD BE ON EVERYONE ELSE. YEAH!
"AND I'VE GOT JUS' THE WAY TO DO IT.
POISON IVY'S GOT A POTION HERE FOR EVERYTHING.
SNIFF SNIFF
HMMM... NOW, WHICH ONE OF THESE WILL DO THE TRICK?

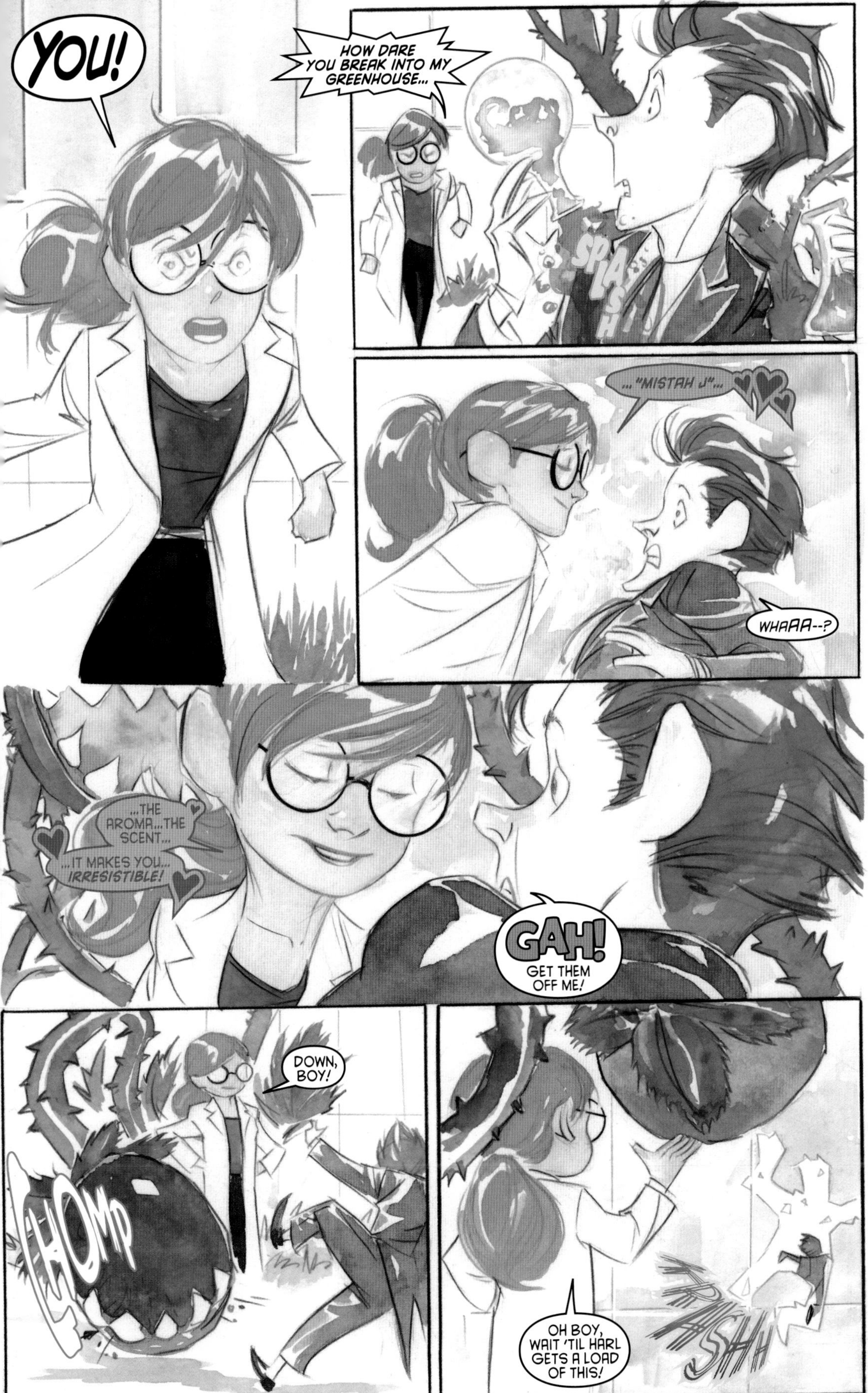
YOU!
HOW DARE YOU BREAK INTO MY GREENHOUSE...
SPLASH!
..."MISTAH J"...
WHAAA--?
...THE AROMA...THE SCENT...
...IT MAKES YOU... IRRESISTIBLE!
GAH! GET THEM OFF ME!
DOWN, BOY!
CHOMP
OH BOY, WAIT 'TIL HARL GETS A LOAD OF THIS!
KRASHH

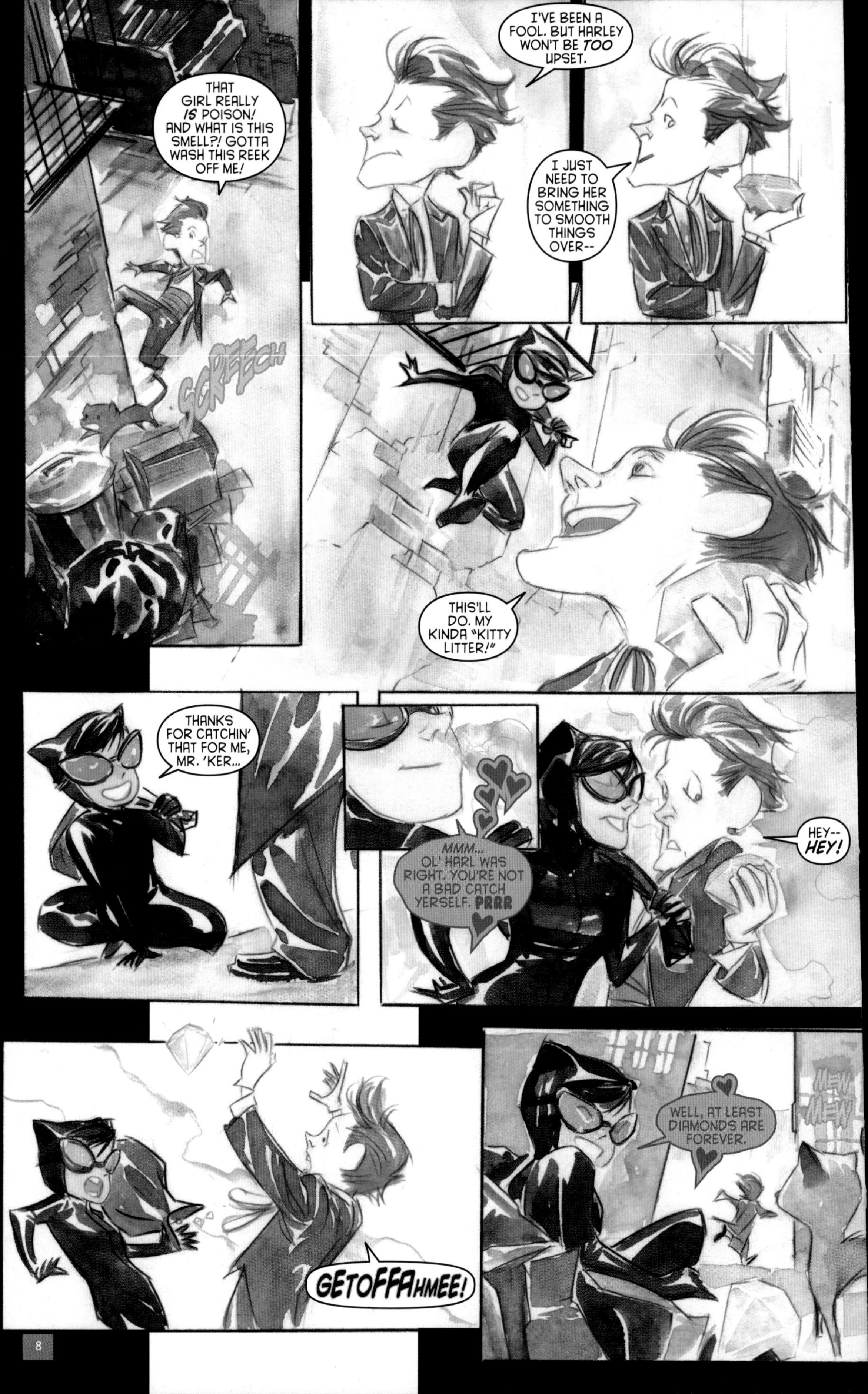
THAT GIRL REALLY *IS* POISON! AND WHAT IS THIS SMELL?! GOTTA WASH THIS REEK OFF ME!
SCREECH
I'VE BEEN A FOOL. BUT HARLEY WON'T BE *TOO* UPSET.
I JUST NEED TO BRING HER SOMETHING TO SMOOTH THINGS OVER--
THIS'LL DO. MY KINDA "KITTY LITTER!"
THANKS FOR CATCHIN' THAT FOR ME, MR. 'KER...
MMM... OL' HARL WAS RIGHT. YOU'RE NOT A BAD CATCH YERSELF. **PRRR**
HEY-- ***HEY!***
GETOFFAHMEE!
MEW MEW
WELL, AT LEAST DIAMONDS ARE FOREVER.

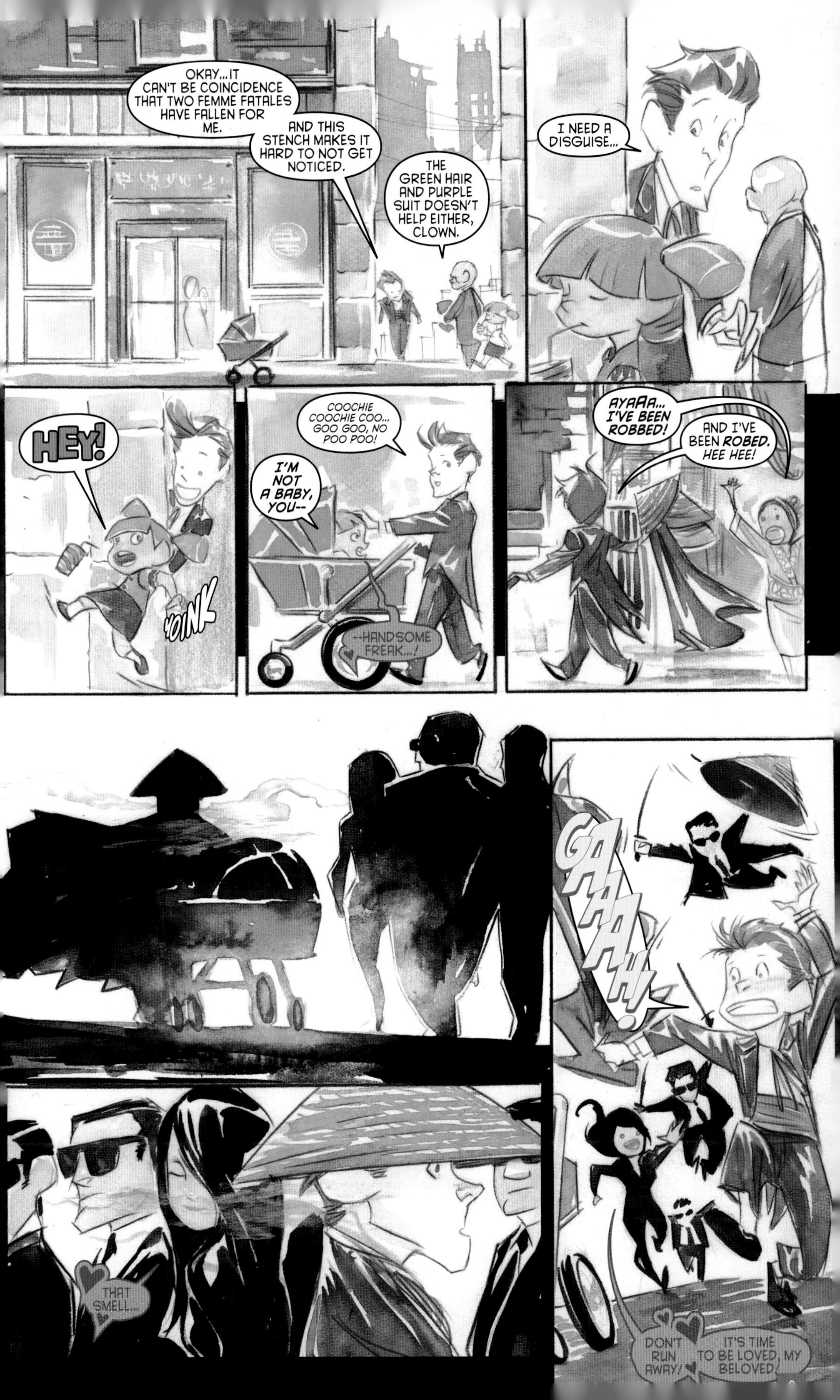
OKAY... IT CAN'T BE COINCIDENCE THAT TWO FEMME FATALES HAVE FALLEN FOR ME.
AND THIS STENCH MAKES IT HARD TO NOT GET NOTICED.
THE GREEN HAIR AND PURPLE SUIT DOESN'T HELP EITHER, CLOWN.
I NEED A DISGUISE...
HEY!
YOINK
COOCHIE COOCHIE COO... GOO GOO, NO POO POO!
I'M NOT A BABY, YOU--
--HANDSOME FREAK...!
AYAAA... I'VE BEEN ROBBED!
AND I'VE BEEN ROBED. HEE HEE!
GAAAAH!
THAT SMELL...
DON'T RUN AWAY!
IT'S TIME TO BE LOVED, MY BELOVED!

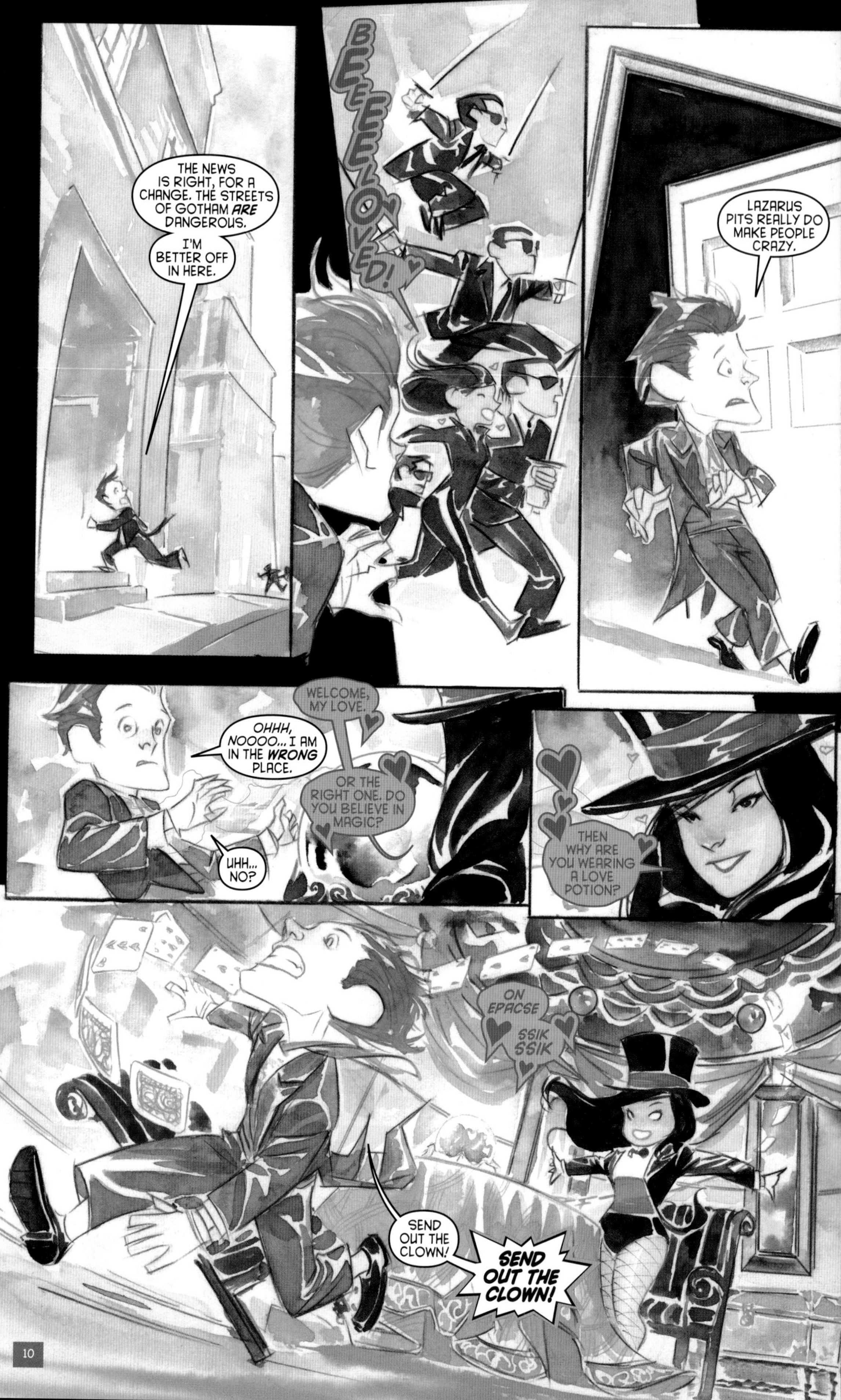
THE NEWS IS RIGHT, FOR A CHANGE. THE STREETS OF GOTHAM *ARE* DANGEROUS.
I'M BETTER OFF IN HERE.
BEEEELOVED!
LAZARUS PITS REALLY DO MAKE PEOPLE CRAZY.
OHHH, NOOOO... I AM IN THE *WRONG* PLACE.
WELCOME, MY LOVE.
OR THE RIGHT ONE. DO YOU BELIEVE IN MAGIC?
UHH... NO?
THEN WHY ARE YOU WEARING A LOVE POTION?
ON EPACSE
SSIK SSIK
SEND OUT THE CLOWN!
SEND OUT THE CLOWN!

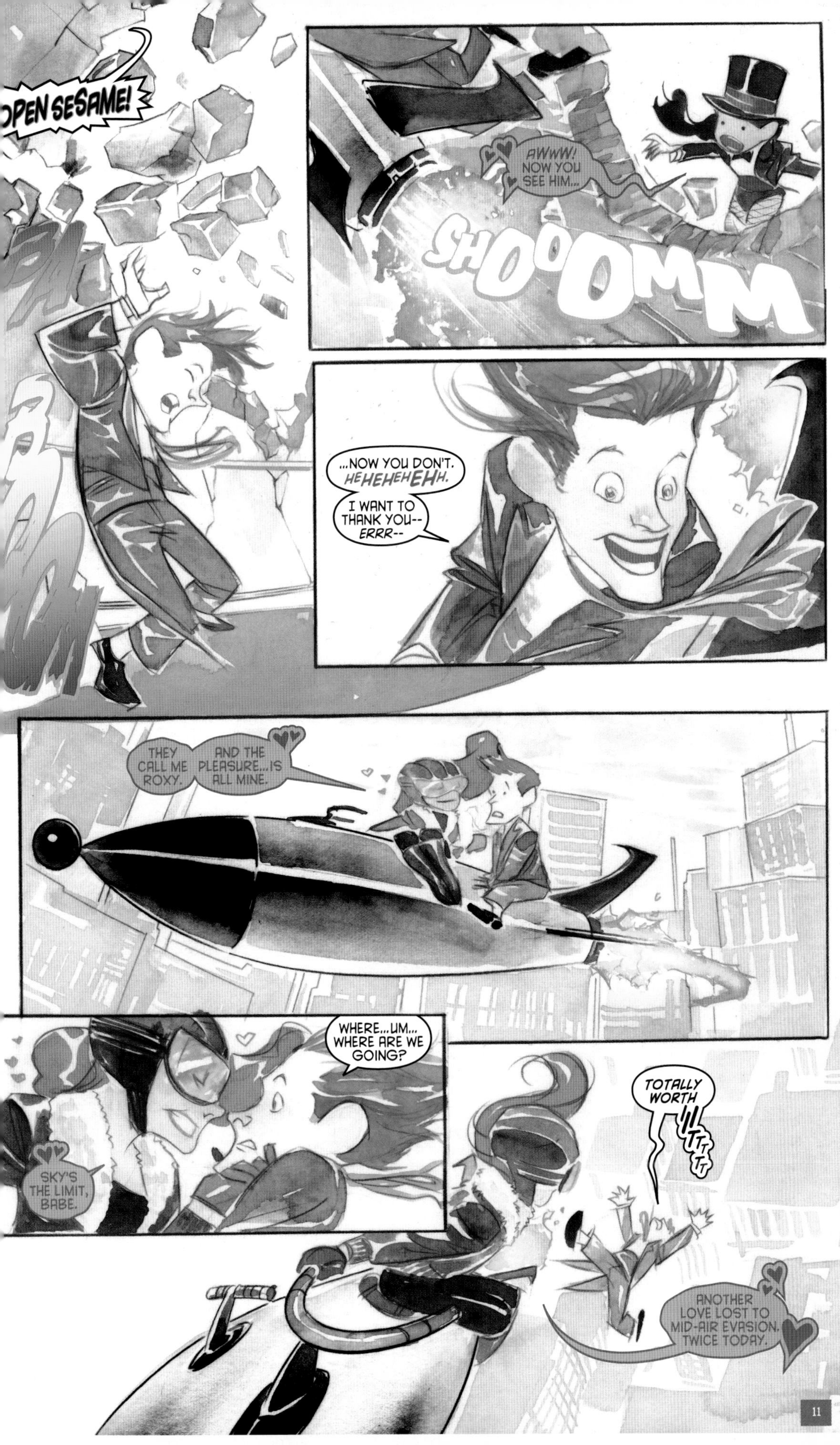
OPEN SESAME!
AWWW! NOW YOU SEE HIM...
SHOOOOMMM
...NOW YOU DON'T. HEHEHEHEHH.
I WANT TO THANK YOU-- ERRR--
THEY CALL ME ROXY.
AND THE PLEASURE...IS ALL MINE.
WHERE...UM... WHERE ARE WE GOING?
SKY'S THE LIMIT, BABE.
TOTALLY WORTH IIITTTTT
ANOTHER LOVE LOST TO MID-AIR EVASION. TWICE TODAY.

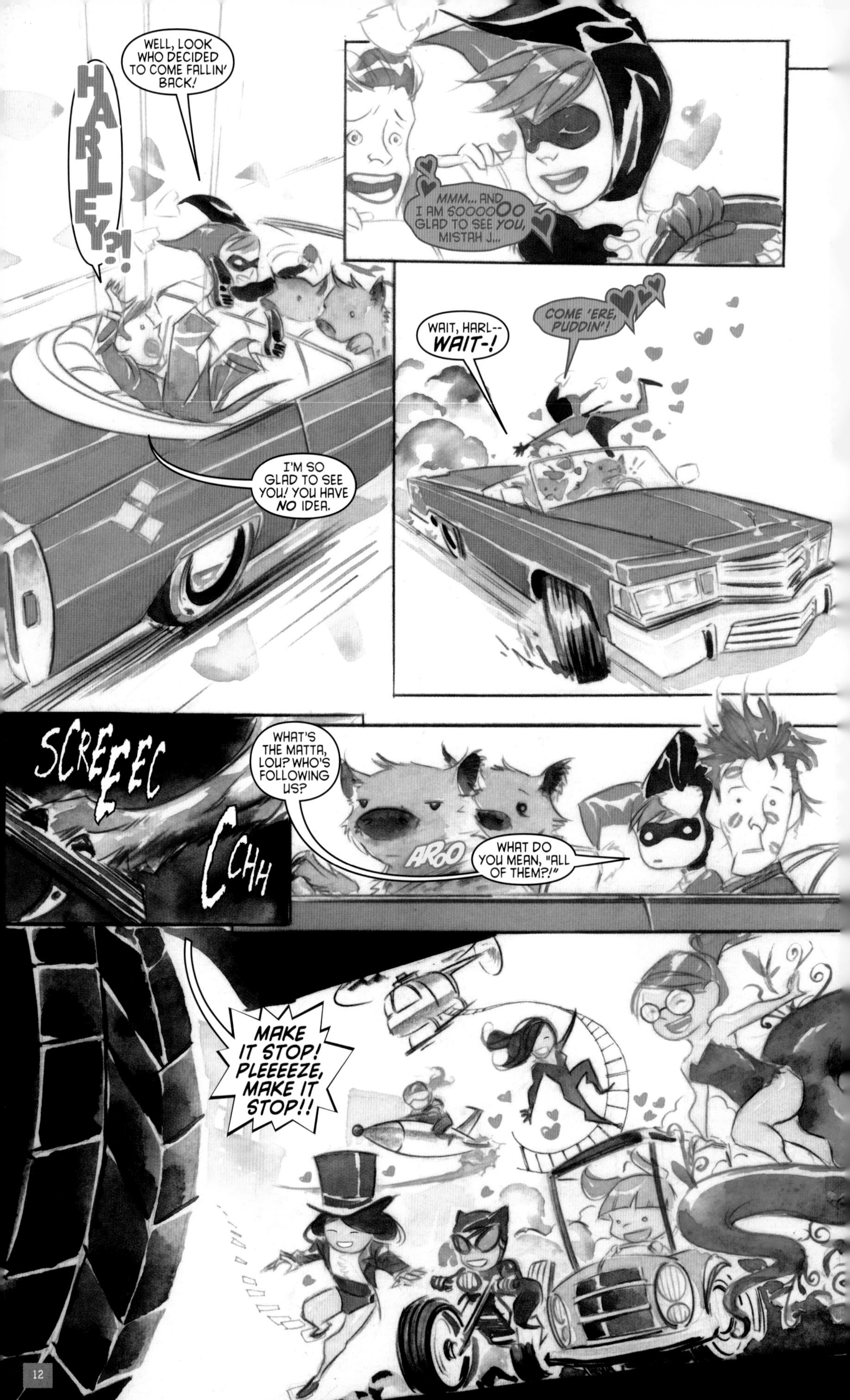
WELL, LOOK WHO DECIDED TO COME FALLIN' BACK!
HARLEY?!!
MMM... AND I AM SOOOOOO GLAD TO SEE YOU, MISTAH J...
I'M SO GLAD TO SEE YOU! YOU HAVE NO IDEA.
WAIT, HARL-- WAIT-!
COME 'ERE, PUDDIN'!
SCREEEC
CCHH
WHAT'S THE MATTA, LOU? WHO'S FOLLOWING US?
AROO
WHAT DO YOU MEAN, "ALL OF THEM?!"
MAKE IT STOP! PLEEEEZE, MAKE IT STOP!!

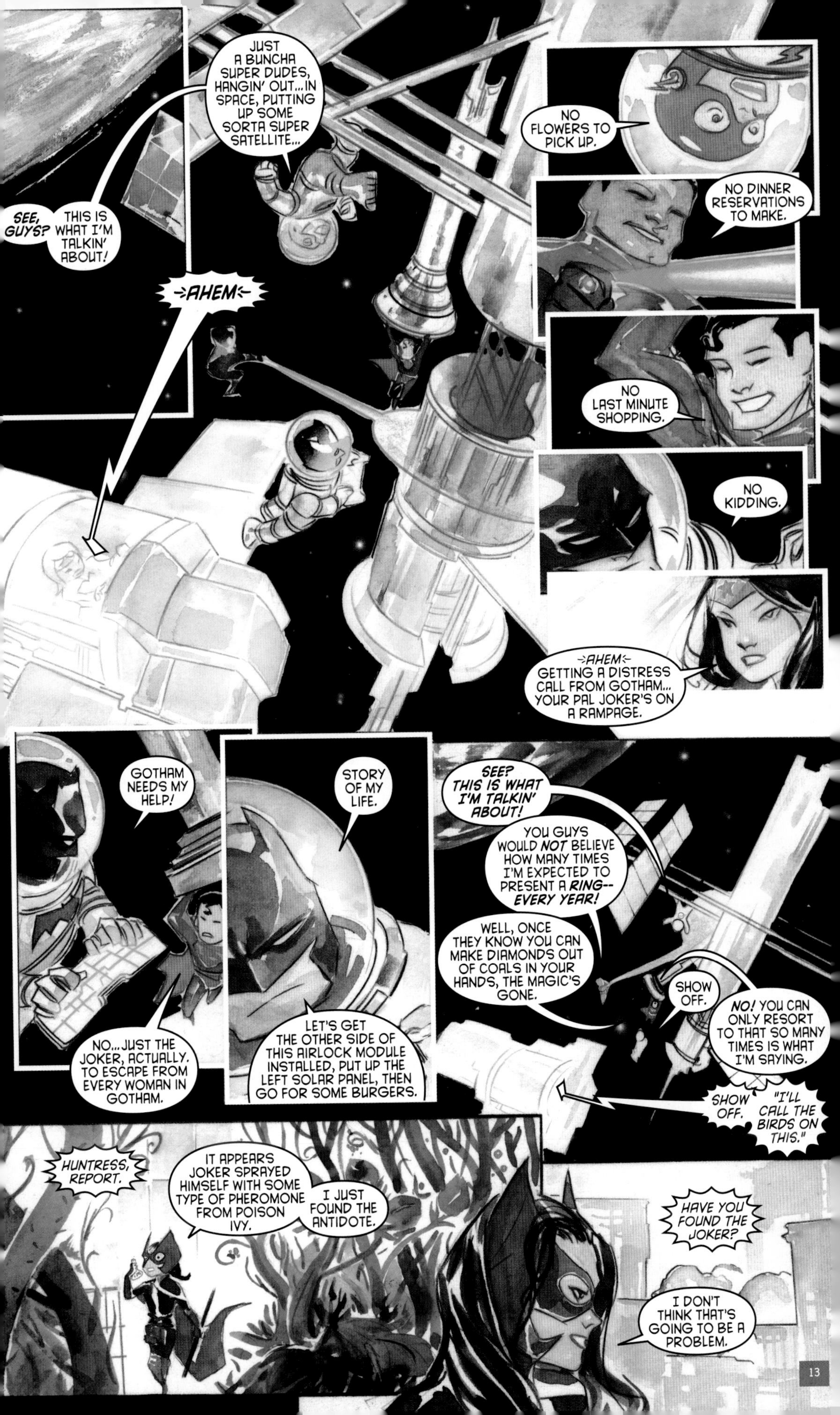

SEE, GUYS?
THIS IS WHAT I'M TALKIN' ABOUT!
JUST A BUNCHA SUPER DUDES, HANGIN' OUT... IN SPACE, PUTTING UP SOME SORTA SUPER SATELLITE...
NO FLOWERS TO PICK UP.
NO DINNER RESERVATIONS TO MAKE.
NO LAST MINUTE SHOPPING.
NO KIDDING.
AHEM
AHEM
GETTING A DISTRESS CALL FROM GOTHAM... YOUR PAL JOKER'S ON A RAMPAGE.
GOTHAM NEEDS MY HELP!
NO... JUST THE JOKER, ACTUALLY. TO ESCAPE FROM EVERY WOMAN IN GOTHAM.
STORY OF MY LIFE.
LET'S GET THE OTHER SIDE OF THIS AIRLOCK MODULE INSTALLED, PUT UP THE LEFT SOLAR PANEL, THEN GO FOR SOME BURGERS.
SEE? THIS IS WHAT I'M TALKIN' ABOUT!
YOU GUYS WOULD NOT BELIEVE HOW MANY TIMES I'M EXPECTED TO PRESENT A RING-- EVERY YEAR!
WELL, ONCE THEY KNOW YOU CAN MAKE DIAMONDS OUT OF COALS IN YOUR HANDS, THE MAGIC'S GONE.
SHOW OFF.
NO! YOU CAN ONLY RESORT TO THAT SO MANY TIMES IS WHAT I'M SAYING.
SHOW OFF.
"I'LL CALL THE BIRDS ON THIS."
HUNTRESS, REPORT.
IT APPEARS JOKER SPRAYED HIMSELF WITH SOME TYPE OF PHEROMONE FROM POISON IVY.
I JUST FOUND THE ANTIDOTE.
HAVE YOU FOUND THE JOKER?
I DON'T THINK THAT'S GOING TO BE A PROBLEM.

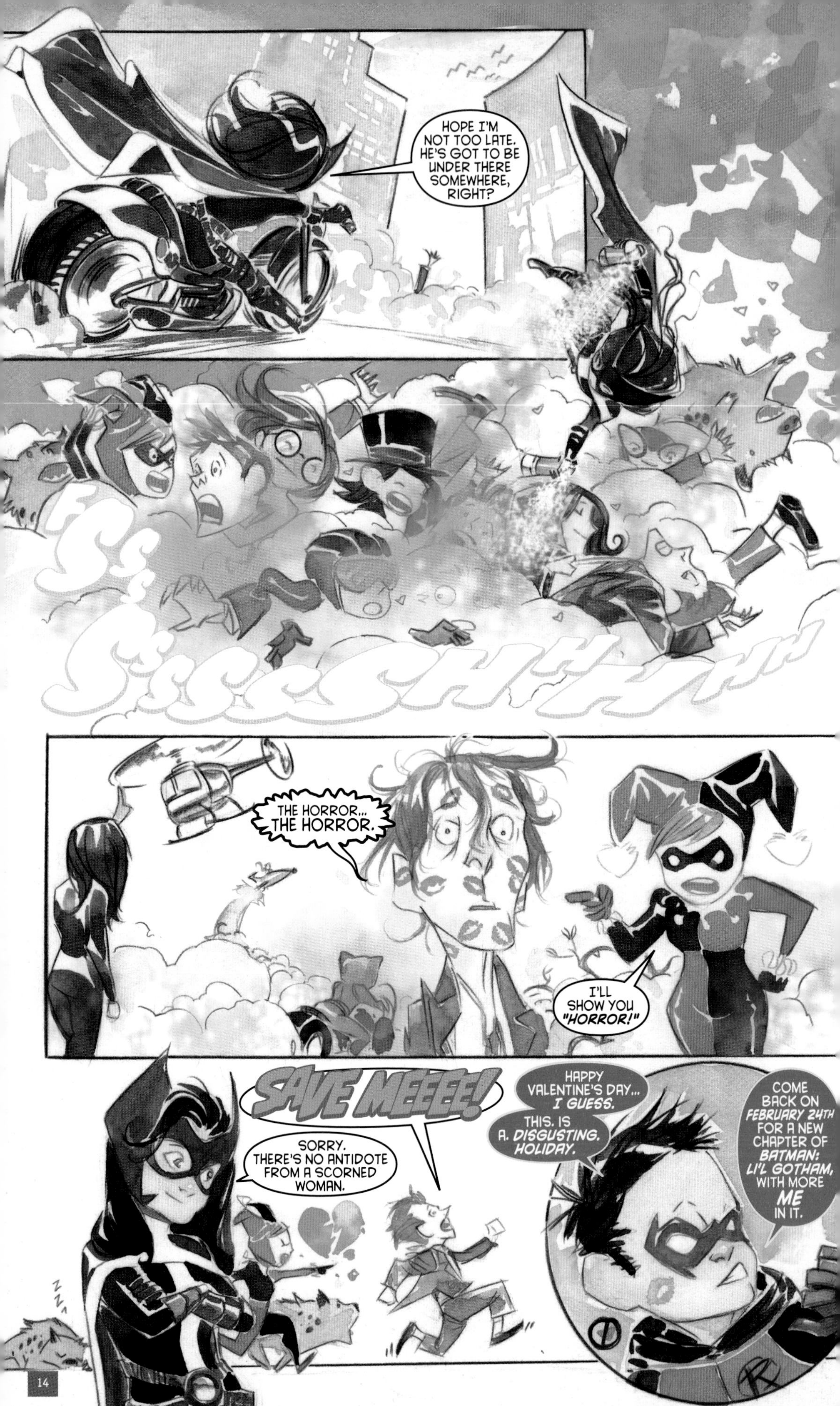
HOPE I'M NOT TOO LATE. HE'S GOT TO BE UNDER THERE SOMEWHERE, RIGHT?
FSSSSSSSHHHHH
THE HORROR... THE HORROR.
I'LL SHOW YOU "HORROR!"
SAVE MEEEE!
SORRY. THERE'S NO ANTIDOTE FROM A SCORNED WOMAN.
HAPPY VALENTINE'S DAY... I GUESS.
THIS. IS A. DISGUSTING. HOLIDAY.
COME BACK ON FEBRUARY 24TH FOR A NEW CHAPTER OF BATMAN: LI'L GOTHAM, WITH MORE ME IN IT.

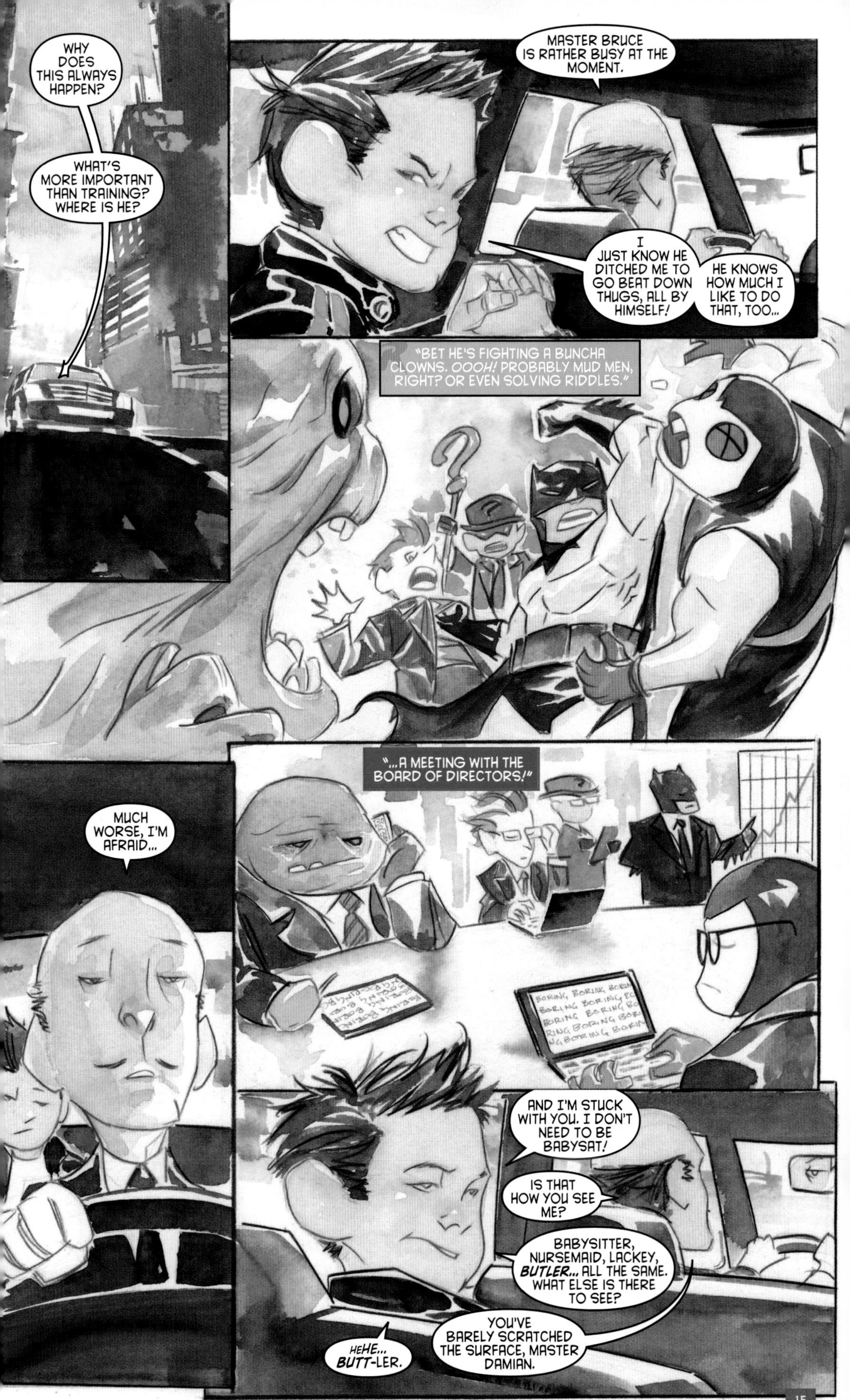
WHY DOES THIS ALWAYS HAPPEN?
WHAT'S MORE IMPORTANT THAN TRAINING? WHERE IS HE?
MASTER BRUCE IS RATHER BUSY AT THE MOMENT.
I JUST KNOW HE DITCHED ME TO GO BEAT DOWN THUGS, ALL BY HIMSELF!
HE KNOWS HOW MUCH I LIKE TO DO THAT, TOO...
"BET HE'S FIGHTING A BUNCHA CLOWNS. *OOOH!* PROBABLY MUD MEN, RIGHT? OR EVEN SOLVING RIDDLES."
MUCH WORSE, I'M AFRAID...
"...A MEETING WITH THE BOARD OF DIRECTORS!"
BORING BORING BORING
AND I'M STUCK WITH YOU. I DON'T NEED TO BE BABYSAT!
IS THAT HOW YOU SEE ME?
BABYSITTER, NURSEMAID, LACKEY, ***BUTLER...*** ALL THE SAME. WHAT ELSE IS THERE TO SEE?
YOU'VE BARELY SCRATCHED THE SURFACE, MASTER DAMIAN.
HEHE... ***BUTT***-LER.

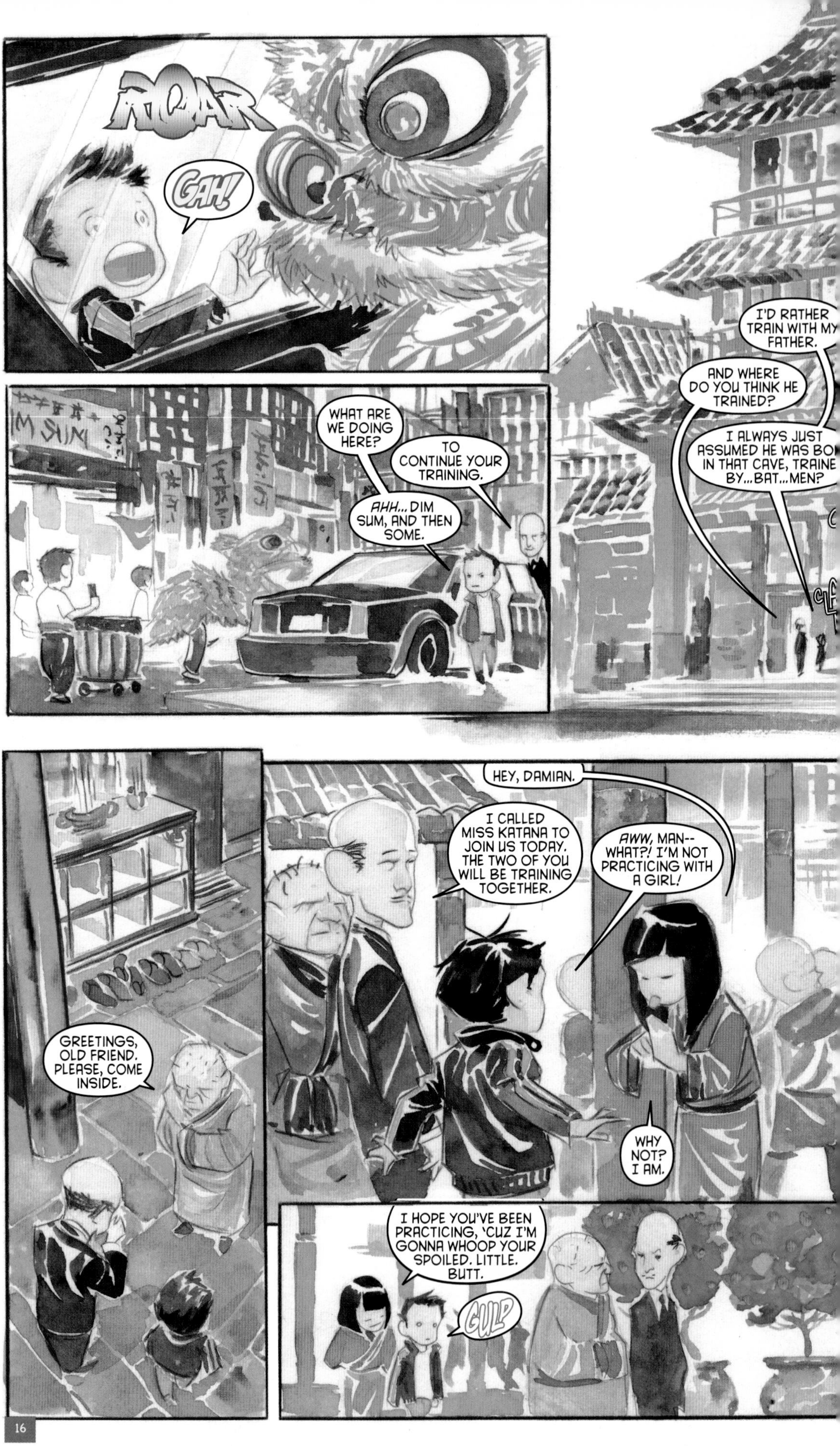
ROAR
GAH!
WHAT ARE WE DOING HERE?
TO CONTINUE YOUR TRAINING.
AHH... DIM SUM, AND THEN SOME.
I'D RATHER TRAIN WITH MY FATHER.
AND WHERE DO YOU THINK HE TRAINED?
I ALWAYS JUST ASSUMED HE WAS BO IN THAT CAVE, TRAINE BY...BAT...MEN?
GREETINGS, OLD FRIEND. PLEASE, COME INSIDE.
HEY, DAMIAN.
I CALLED MISS KATANA TO JOIN US TODAY. THE TWO OF YOU WILL BE TRAINING TOGETHER.
AWW, MAN-- WHAT?! I'M NOT PRACTICING WITH A GIRL!
WHY NOT? I AM.
I HOPE YOU'VE BEEN PRACTICING, 'CUZ I'M GONNA WHOOP YOUR SPOILED. LITTLE. BUTT.
GULP

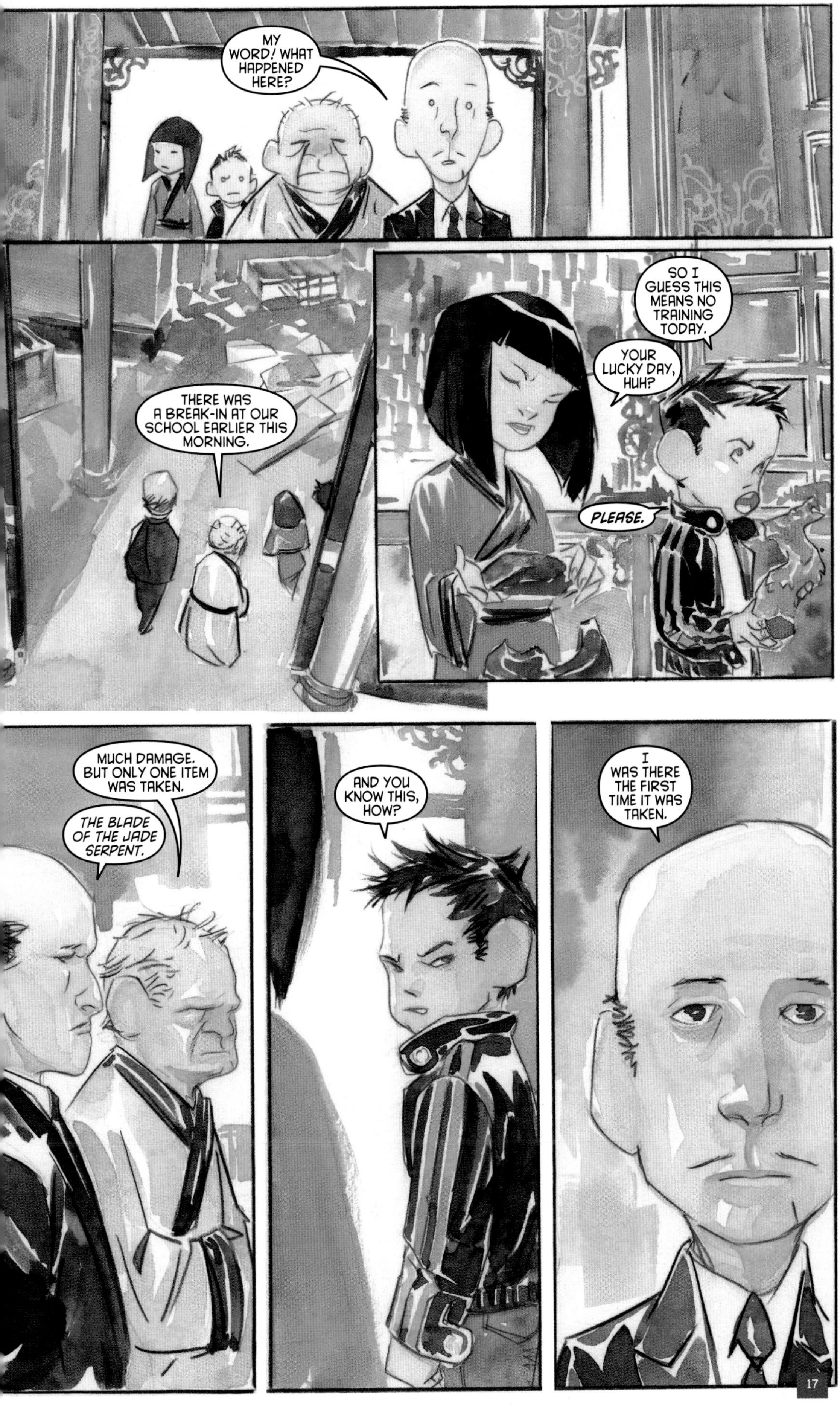
MY WORD! WHAT HAPPENED HERE?
THERE WAS A BREAK-IN AT OUR SCHOOL EARLIER THIS MORNING.
SO I GUESS THIS MEANS NO TRAINING TODAY.
YOUR LUCKY DAY, HUH?
PLEASE.
MUCH DAMAGE. BUT ONLY ONE ITEM WAS TAKEN.
THE BLADE OF THE JADE SERPENT.
AND YOU KNOW THIS, HOW?
I WAS THERE THE FIRST TIME IT WAS TAKEN.

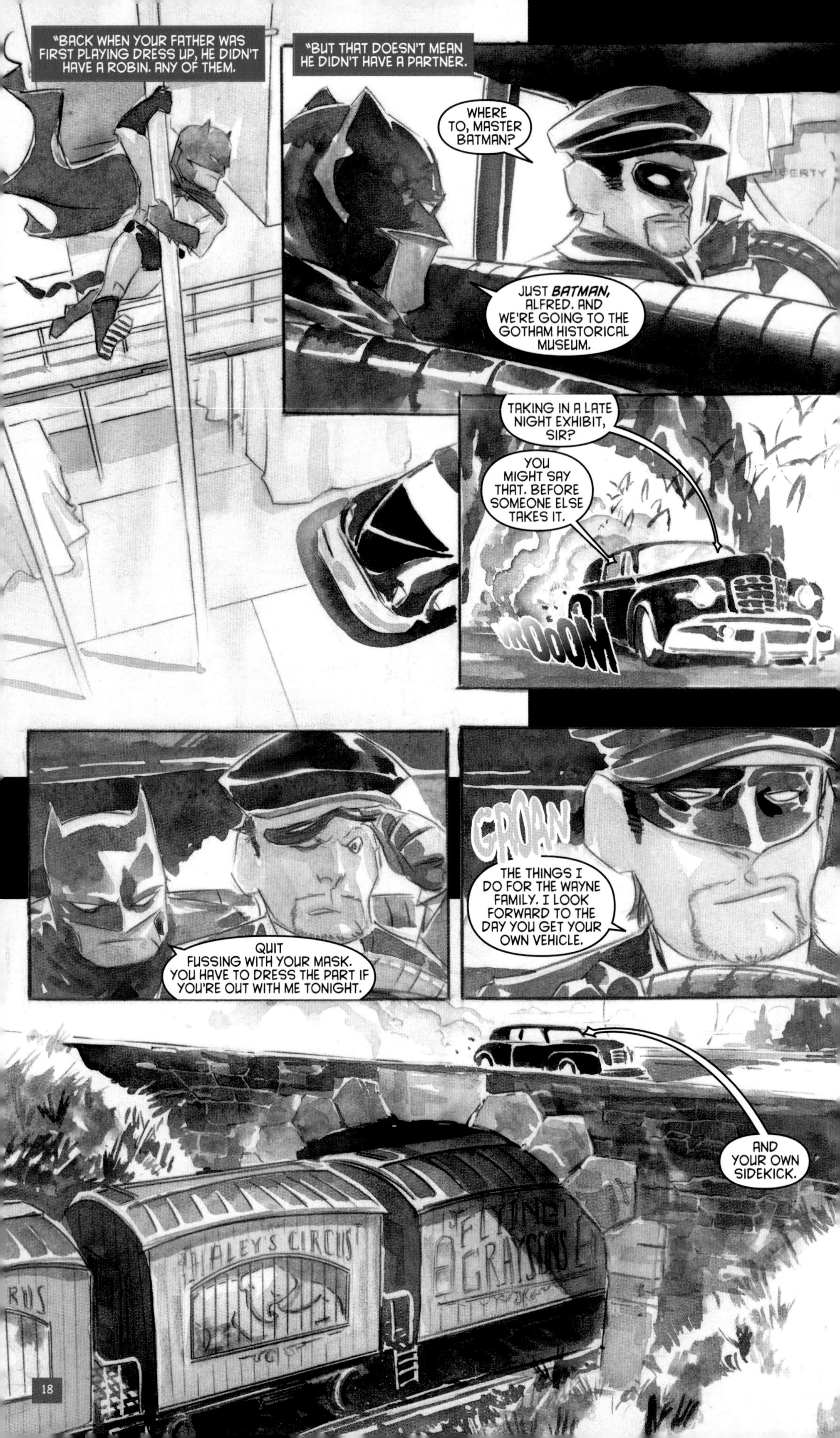
"BACK WHEN YOUR FATHER WAS FIRST PLAYING DRESS UP, HE DIDN'T HAVE A ROBIN. ANY OF THEM.
"BUT THAT DOESN'T MEAN HE DIDN'T HAVE A PARTNER.
WHERE TO, MASTER BATMAN?
JUST **BATMAN,** ALFRED. AND WE'RE GOING TO THE GOTHAM HISTORICAL MUSEUM.
TAKING IN A LATE NIGHT EXHIBIT, SIR?
YOU MIGHT SAY THAT. BEFORE SOMEONE ELSE TAKES IT.
VROOOOM
QUIT FUSSING WITH YOUR MASK. YOU HAVE TO DRESS THE PART IF YOU'RE OUT WITH ME TONIGHT.
GROAN
THE THINGS I DO FOR THE WAYNE FAMILY. I LOOK FORWARD TO THE DAY YOU GET YOUR OWN VEHICLE.
AND YOUR OWN SIDEKICK.
HALEY'S CIRCUS
FLYING GRAYSONS

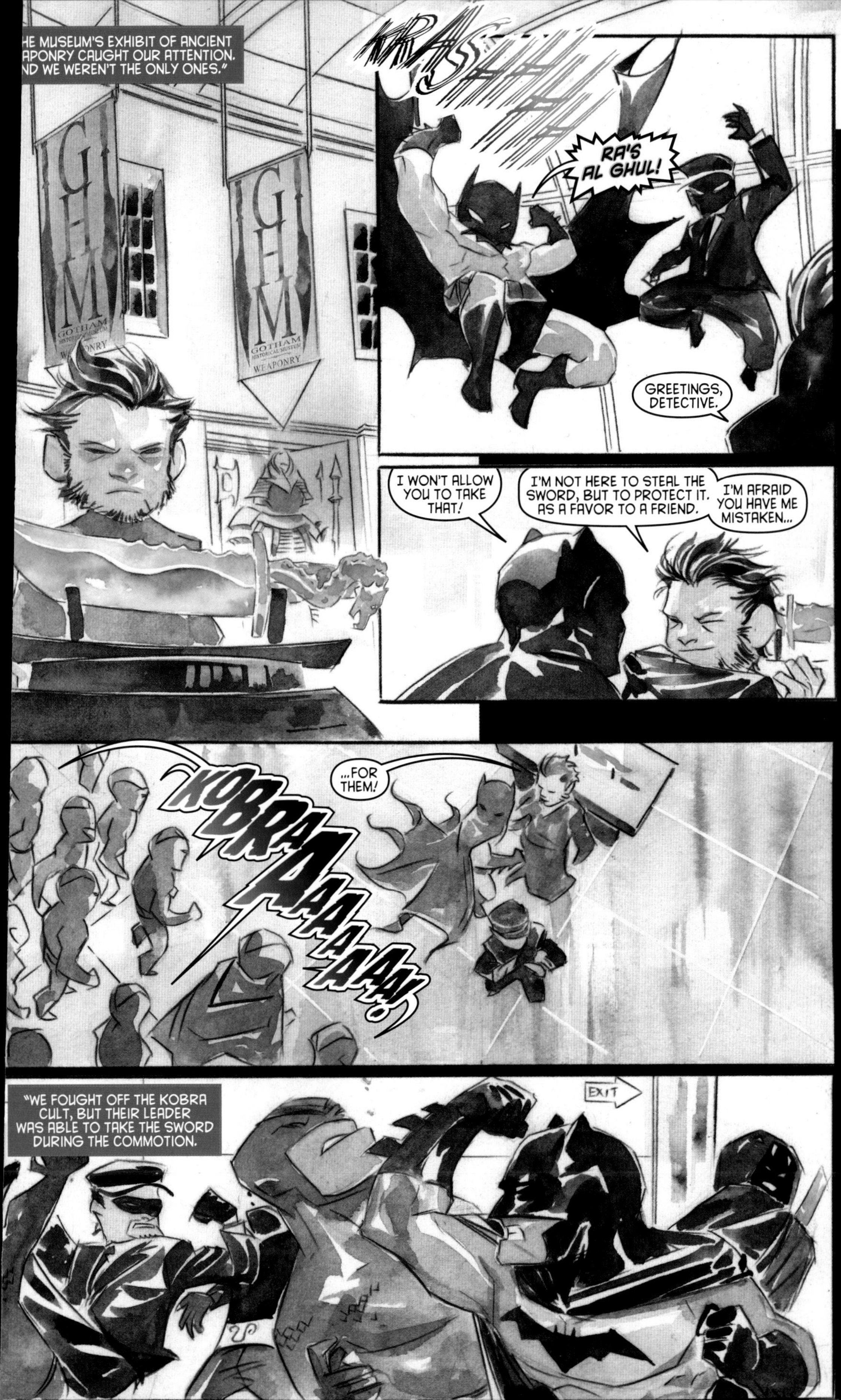
HE MUSEUM'S EXHIBIT OF ANCIENT
APONRY CAUGHT OUR ATTENTION.
ND WE WEREN'T THE ONLY ONES."
GHM
GOTHAM
WEAPONRY
RA'S AL GHUL!
GREETINGS, DETECTIVE.
I WON'T ALLOW YOU TO TAKE THAT!
I'M NOT HERE TO STEAL THE SWORD, BUT TO PROTECT IT. AS A FAVOR TO A FRIEND.
I'M AFRAID YOU HAVE ME MISTAKEN...
...FOR THEM!
KOBRAAAAAAA!
"WE FOUGHT OFF THE KOBRA CULT, BUT THEIR LEADER WAS ABLE TO TAKE THE SWORD DURING THE COMMOTION.
EXIT

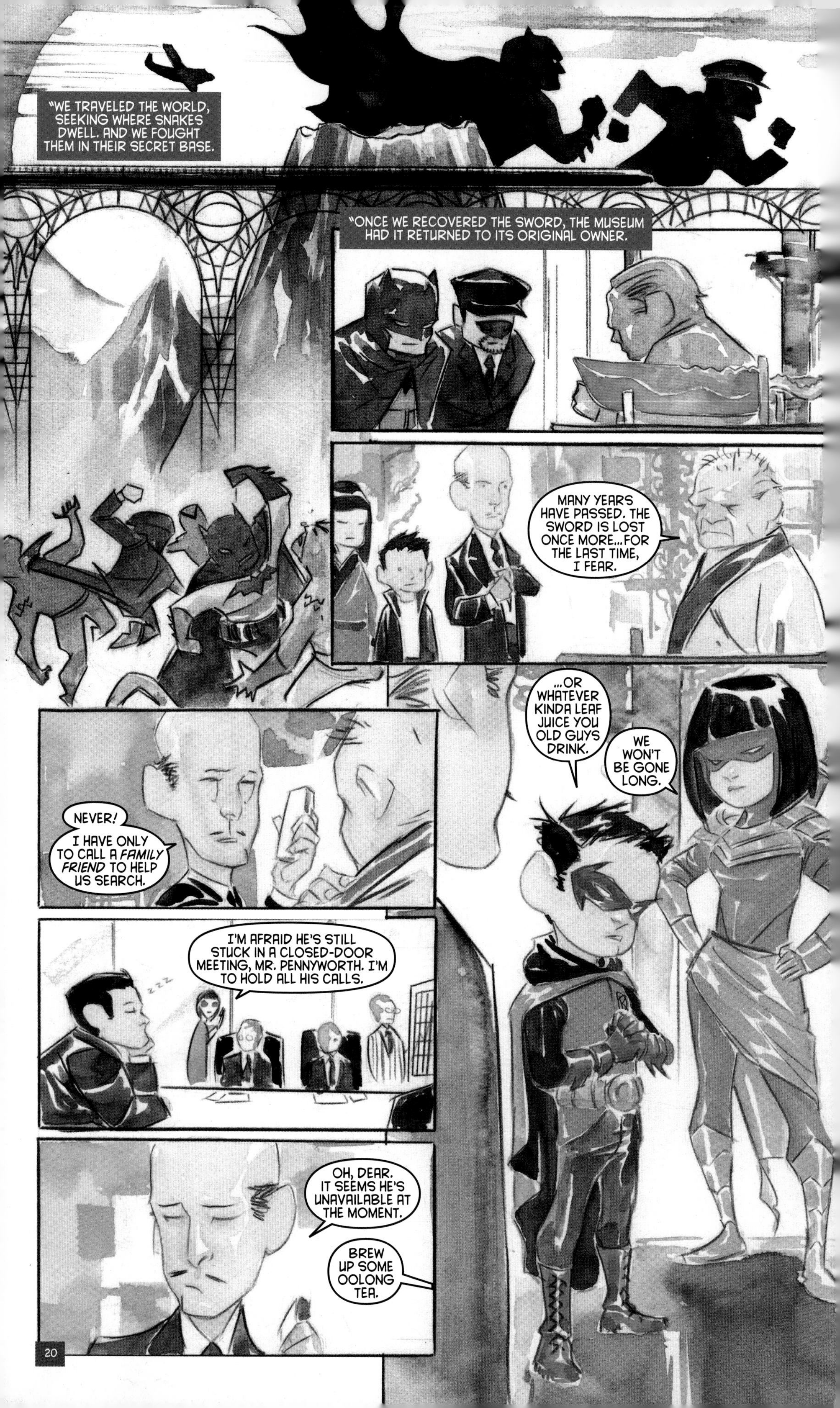

"WE TRAVELED THE WORLD, SEEKING WHERE SNAKES DWELL. AND WE FOUGHT THEM IN THEIR SECRET BASE.
"ONCE WE RECOVERED THE SWORD, THE MUSEUM HAD IT RETURNED TO ITS ORIGINAL OWNER.
MANY YEARS HAVE PASSED. THE SWORD IS LOST ONCE MORE... FOR THE LAST TIME, I FEAR.
NEVER!
I HAVE ONLY TO CALL A *FAMILY FRIEND* TO HELP US SEARCH.
I'M AFRAID HE'S STILL STUCK IN A CLOSED-DOOR MEETING, MR. PENNYWORTH. I'M TO HOLD ALL HIS CALLS.
OH, DEAR. IT SEEMS HE'S UNAVAILABLE AT THE MOMENT.
BREW UP SOME OOLONG TEA.
...OR WHATEVER KINDA LEAF JUICE YOU OLD GUYS DRINK.
WE WON'T BE GONE LONG.

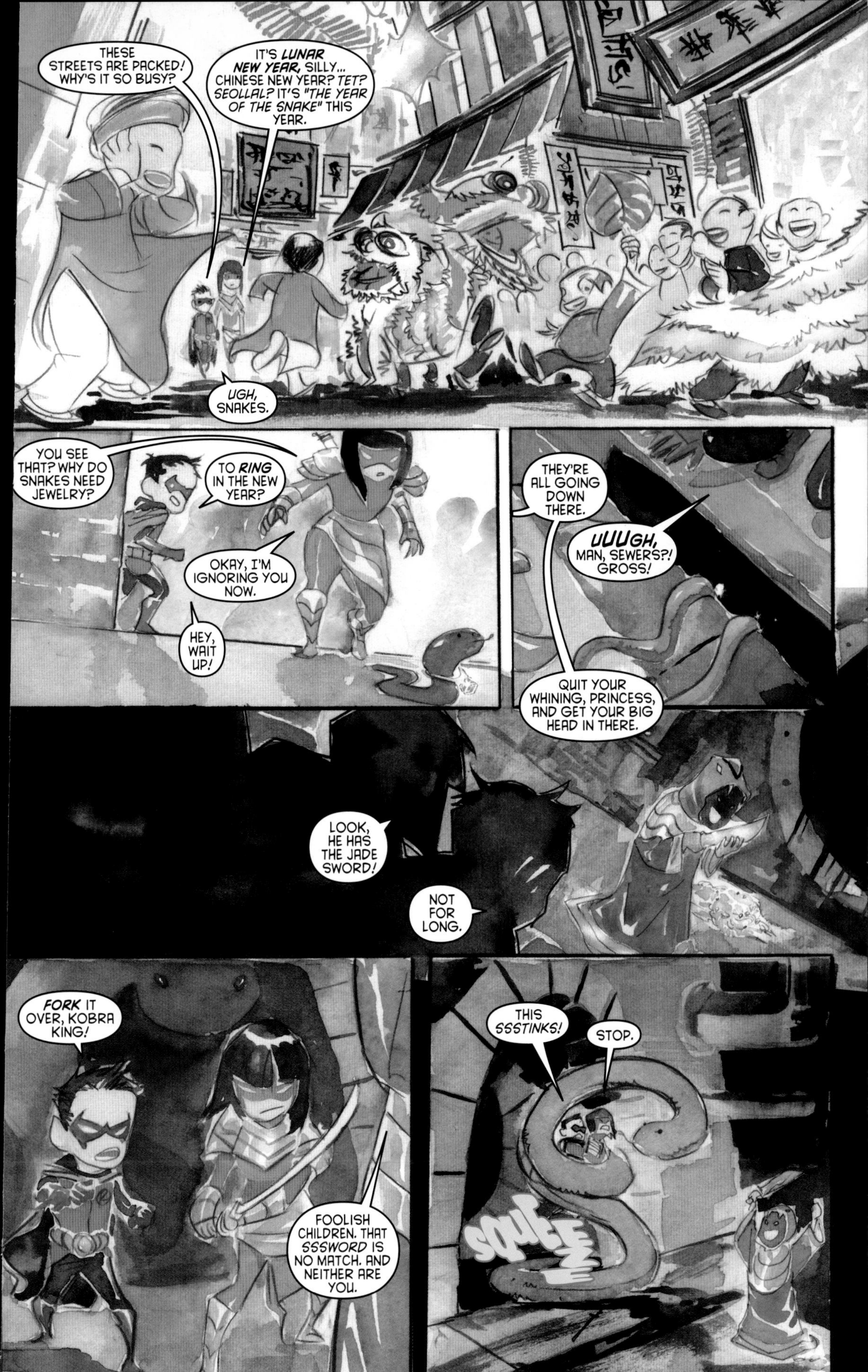
THESE STREETS ARE PACKED! WHY'S IT SO BUSY?
IT'S LUNAR NEW YEAR, SILLY... CHINESE NEW YEAR? TET? SEOLLAL? IT'S "THE YEAR OF THE SNAKE" THIS YEAR.
UGH, SNAKES.
YOU SEE THAT? WHY DO SNAKES NEED JEWELRY?
TO RING IN THE NEW YEAR?
OKAY, I'M IGNORING YOU NOW.
HEY, WAIT UP!
THEY'RE ALL GOING DOWN THERE.
UUUGH, MAN, SEWERS?! GROSS!
QUIT YOUR WHINING, PRINCESS, AND GET YOUR BIG HEAD IN THERE.
LOOK, HE HAS THE JADE SWORD!
NOT FOR LONG.
FORK IT OVER, KOBRA KING!
FOOLISH CHILDREN. THAT SSSWORD IS NO MATCH. AND NEITHER ARE YOU.
THIS SSSTINKS!
STOP.
SQUEEEM

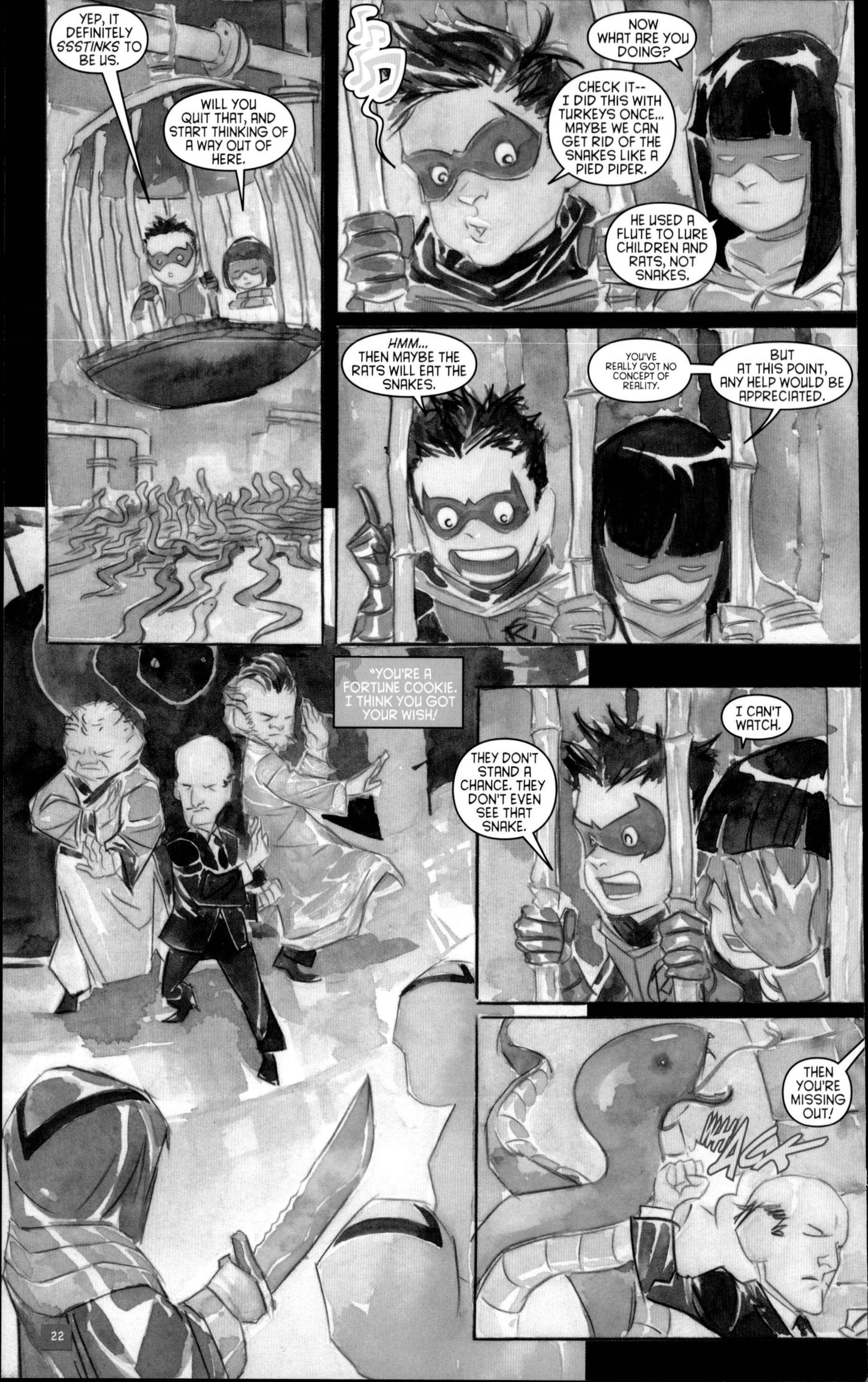
YEP, IT DEFINITELY SSSTINKS TO BE US.
WILL YOU QUIT THAT, AND START THINKING OF A WAY OUT OF HERE.
NOW WHAT ARE YOU DOING?
CHECK IT-- I DID THIS WITH TURKEYS ONCE... MAYBE WE CAN GET RID OF THE SNAKES LIKE A PIED PIPER.
HE USED A FLUTE TO LURE CHILDREN AND RATS, NOT SNAKES.
HMM... THEN MAYBE THE RATS WILL EAT THE SNAKES.
YOU'VE REALLY GOT NO CONCEPT OF REALITY.
BUT AT THIS POINT, ANY HELP WOULD BE APPRECIATED.
"YOU'RE A FORTUNE COOKIE. I THINK YOU GOT YOUR WISH!
THEY DON'T STAND A CHANCE. THEY DON'T EVEN SEE THAT SNAKE.
I CAN'T WATCH.
THEN YOU'RE MISSING OUT!
THWACK

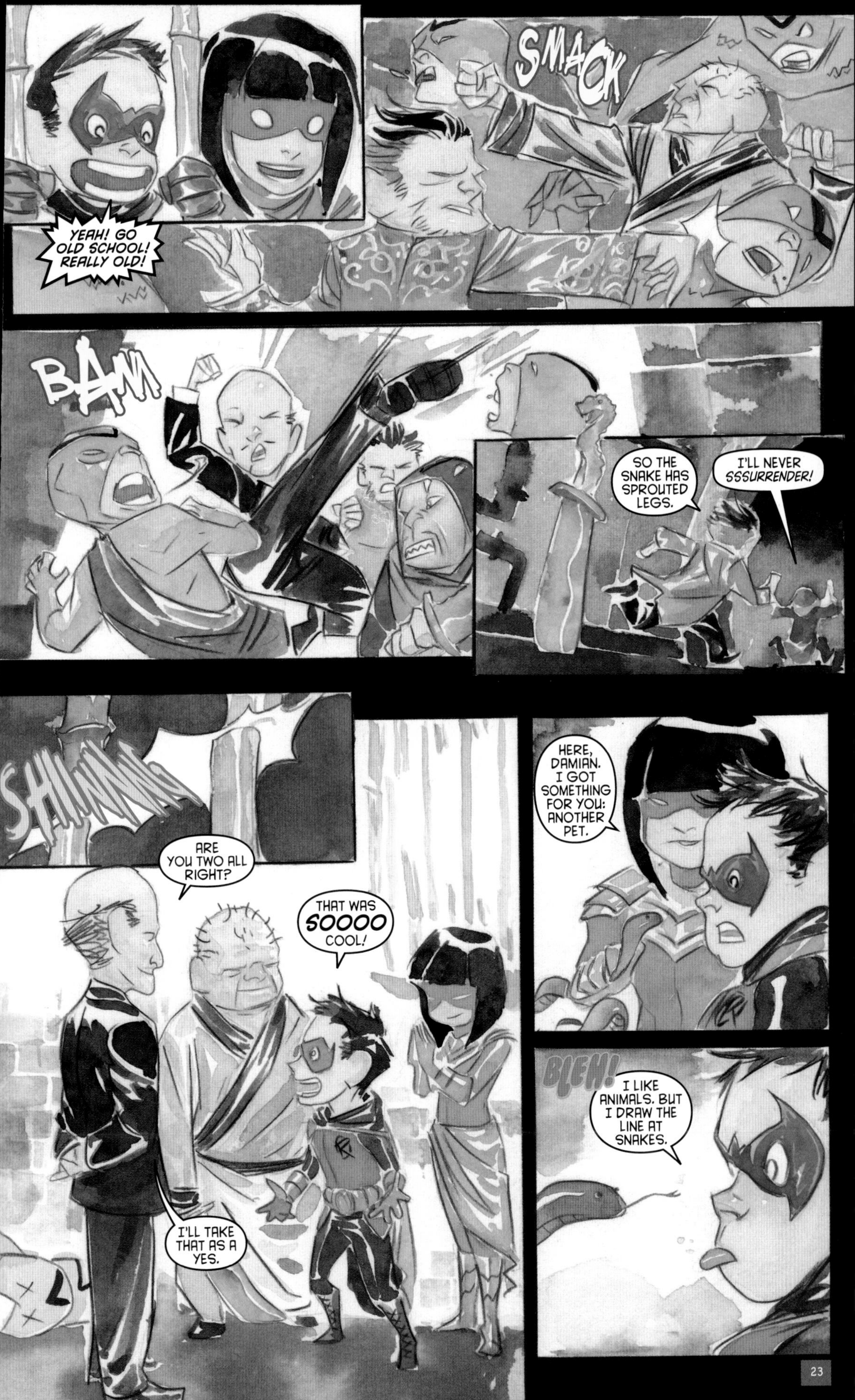

SMACK
YEAH! GO OLD SCHOOL! REALLY OLD!
BAM
SO THE SNAKE HAS SPROUTED LEGS.
I'LL NEVER SSSURRENDER!
SHHNNN
ARE YOU TWO ALL RIGHT?
THAT WAS SOOOO COOL!
I'LL TAKE THAT AS A YES.
HERE, DAMIAN. I GOT SOMETHING FOR YOU: ANOTHER PET.
BLEH!
I LIKE ANIMALS. BUT I DRAW THE LINE AT SNAKES.

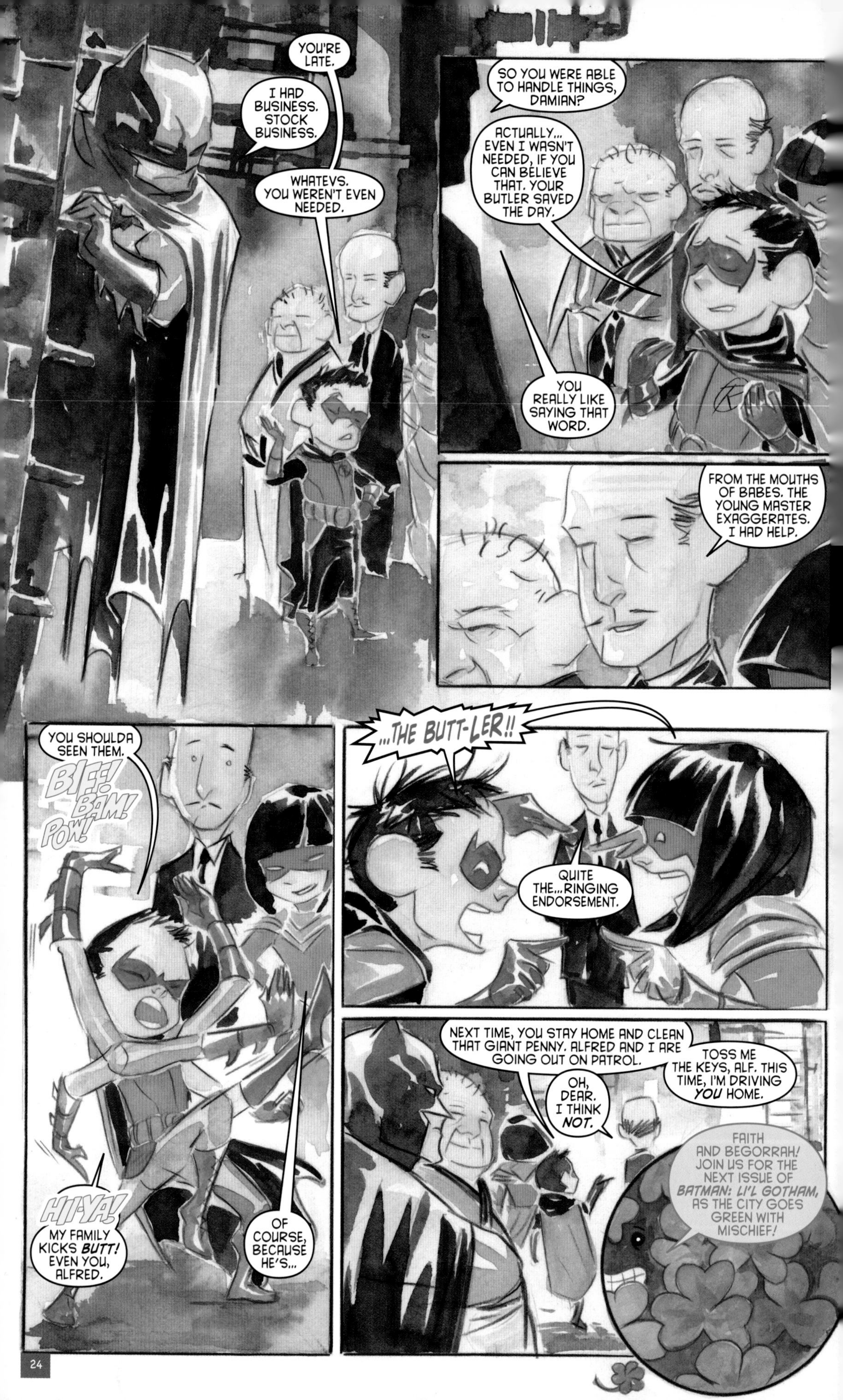
YOU'RE LATE.
I HAD BUSINESS. STOCK BUSINESS.
WHATEVS. YOU WEREN'T EVEN NEEDED.
SO YOU WERE ABLE TO HANDLE THINGS, DAMIAN?
ACTUALLY... EVEN I WASN'T NEEDED, IF YOU CAN BELIEVE THAT. YOUR BUTLER SAVED THE DAY.
YOU REALLY LIKE SAYING THAT WORD.
FROM THE MOUTHS OF BABES. THE YOUNG MASTER EXAGGERATES. I HAD HELP.
YOU SHOULDA SEEN THEM.
BIFF! BAM! POW!
HI-YA!
MY FAMILY KICKS BUTT! EVEN YOU, ALFRED.
OF COURSE, BECAUSE HE'S...
...THE BUTT-LER!!
QUITE THE...RINGING ENDORSEMENT.
NEXT TIME, YOU STAY HOME AND CLEAN THAT GIANT PENNY. ALFRED AND I ARE GOING OUT ON PATROL.
TOSS ME THE KEYS, ALF. THIS TIME, I'M DRIVING YOU HOME.
OH, DEAR. I THINK NOT.
FAITH AND BEGORRAH! JOIN US FOR THE NEXT ISSUE OF BATMAN: LI'L GOTHAM, AS THE CITY GOES GREEN WITH MISCHIEF!

CREATORS

DUSTIN NGUYEN — CO-WRITER & ILLUSTRATOR

Dustin Nguyen is an American comic artist whose body of work includes Wildcats v3.0, The Authority Revolution, Batman, Superman/Batman, Detective Comics, Batgirl, and his creator owned project Manifest Eternity. Currently, he produces all the art for Batman: Li'l Gotham, which is also written by himself and Derek Fridolfs. Outside of comics, Dustin moonlights as a conceptual artist for toys, games, and animation. In his spare time, he enjoys sleeping, driving, and sketching things he loves.

DEREK FRIDOLFS — CO-WRITER

Derek Fridolfs is a comic book writer, inker, and artist. He resides in Gotham--present and future.

GLOSSARY

antidote (AN-tuh-dote)--a remedy to counteract the effects of poison

aroma (ah-ROME-uh)--a noticeable and usually pleasant smell

commotion (kuh-MOH-shuhn)--noisy excitement and confusion

concept (CON-sept)--a general idea

disguise (diss-GIZE)--a disguise makes you look like someone or something else

dread (DRED)--to fear greatly

evasion (i-VAY-zhuhn)--the act of getting away from someone or avoiding something

irresistable (ear-uh-ZISS-tuh-buhl)--extremely tempting, or impossible to withstand

Lazarus Pit (LAZZ-er-uhss PITZ)--a mysterious fluid-filled pit in the earth that regenerates and even revives the dead or dying. The lazarus pit is used by the League of Assassins, which Damian a.k.a. Robin used to be a member of.

potion (POH-shuhn)--a mixture of liquids that has an intended effect

triumphant (try-UM-fuhnt)--victorious, or rejoicing in victory

VISUAL QUESTIONS & PROMPTS

1. Why does Robin have several arms in this panel? Why was he drawn this way?

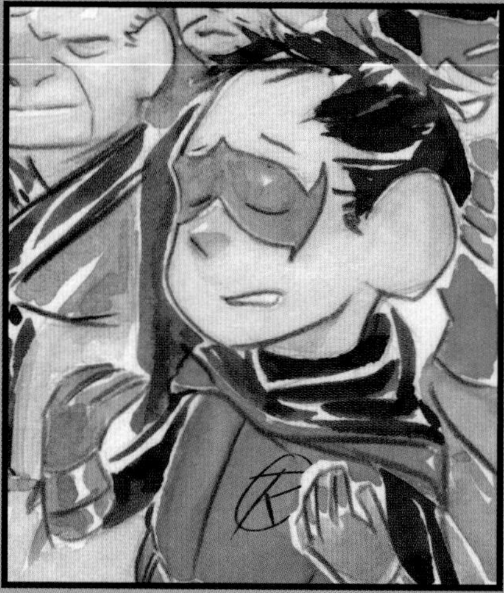

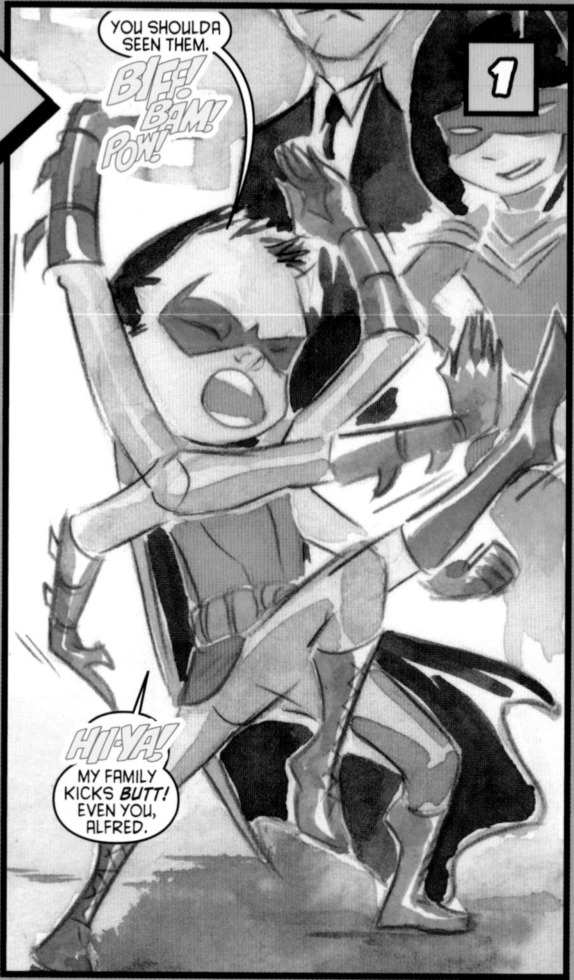
1
YOU SHOULDA SEEN THEM.
BIFF! BAM! POW!
HI-YA!
MY FAMILY KICKS *BUTT!* EVEN YOU, ALFRED.

2. Why is Katana's text in her first speech bubble smaller than normal?

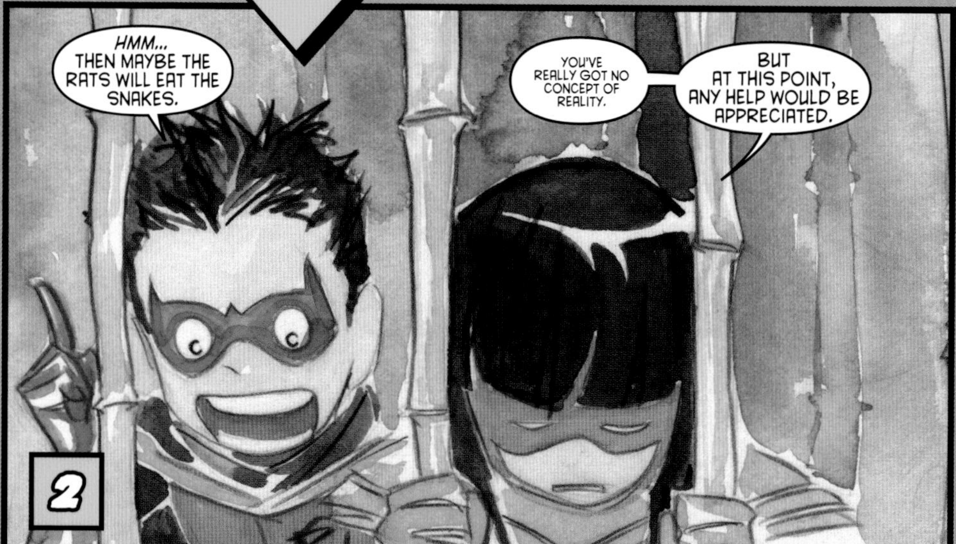
HMM... THEN MAYBE THE RATS WILL EAT THE SNAKES.
YOU'VE REALLY GOT NO CONCEPT OF REALITY.
BUT AT THIS POINT, ANY HELP WOULD BE APPRECIATED.
2

3. These panels are less colorful than the rest of the book. Why does this page look different than the rest of the pages?

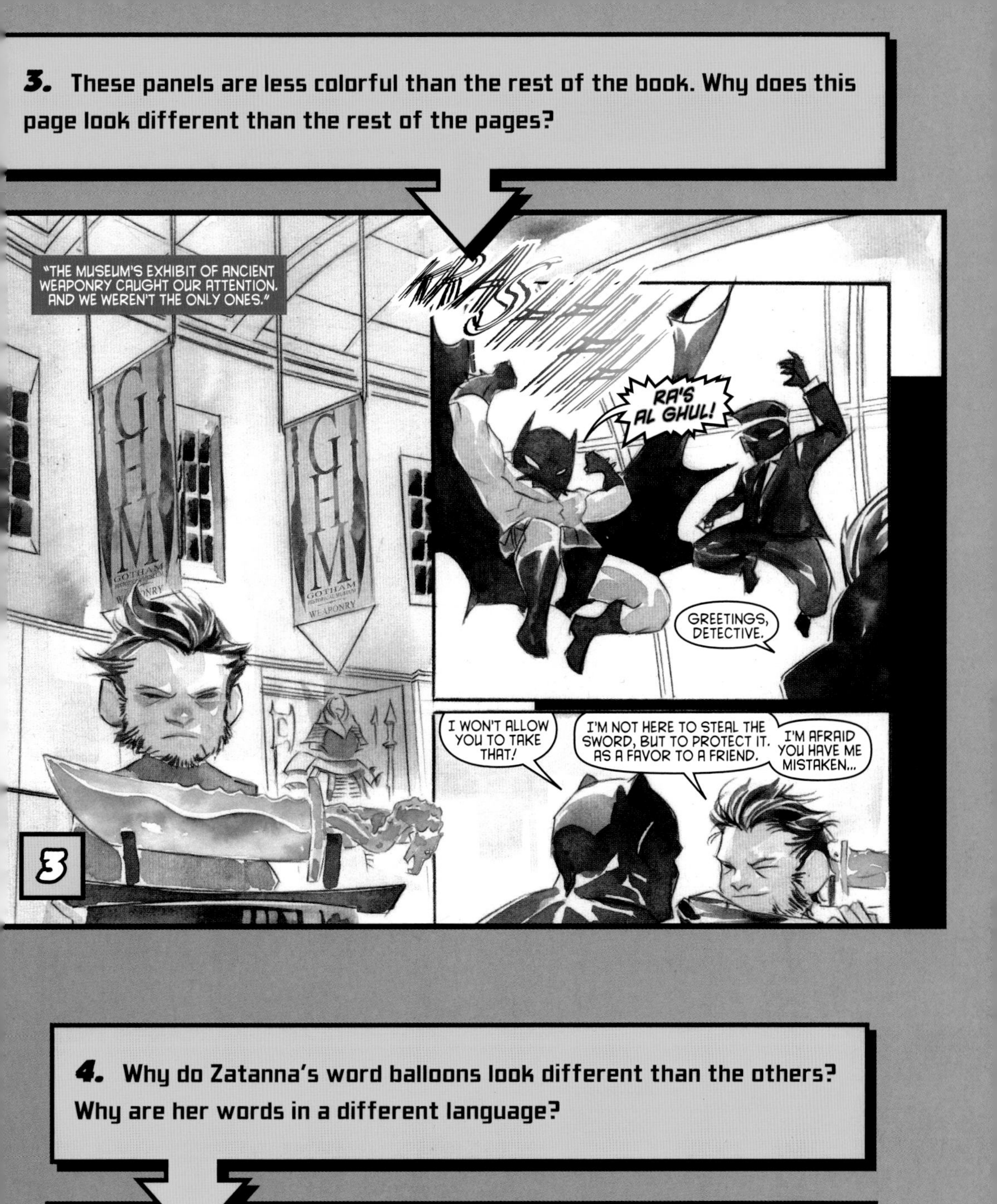
"THE MUSEUM'S EXHIBIT OF ANCIENT WEAPONRY CAUGHT OUR ATTENTION. AND WE WEREN'T THE ONLY ONES."
RA'S AL GHUL!
GREETINGS, DETECTIVE.
I WON'T ALLOW YOU TO TAKE THAT!
I'M AFRAID YOU HAVE ME MISTAKEN...
I'M NOT HERE TO STEAL THE SWORD, BUT TO PROTECT IT. AS A FAVOR TO A FRIEND.
3

4. Why do Zatanna's word balloons look different than the others? Why are her words in a different language?

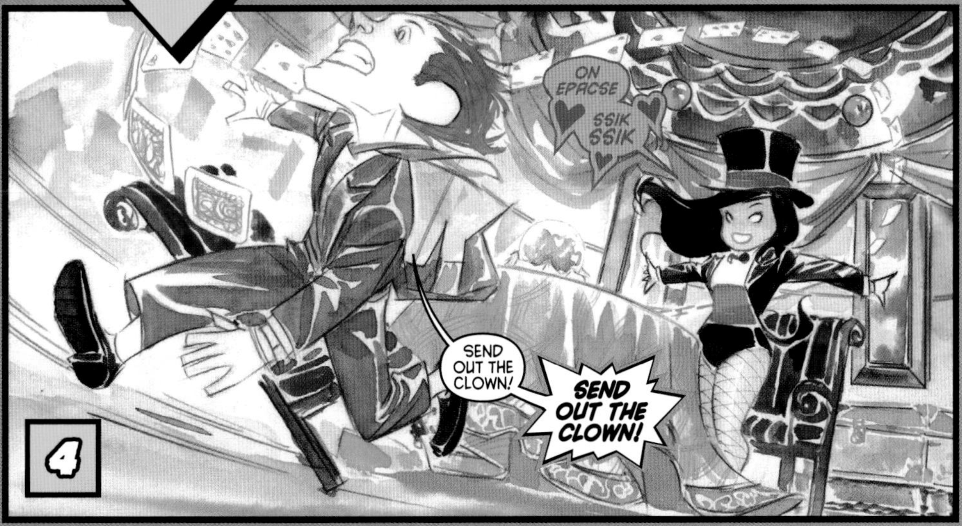
ON EPACSE
SSIK SSIK
SEND OUT THE CLOWN!
SEND OUT THE CLOWN!
4

BATMAN™ LI'L GOTHAM

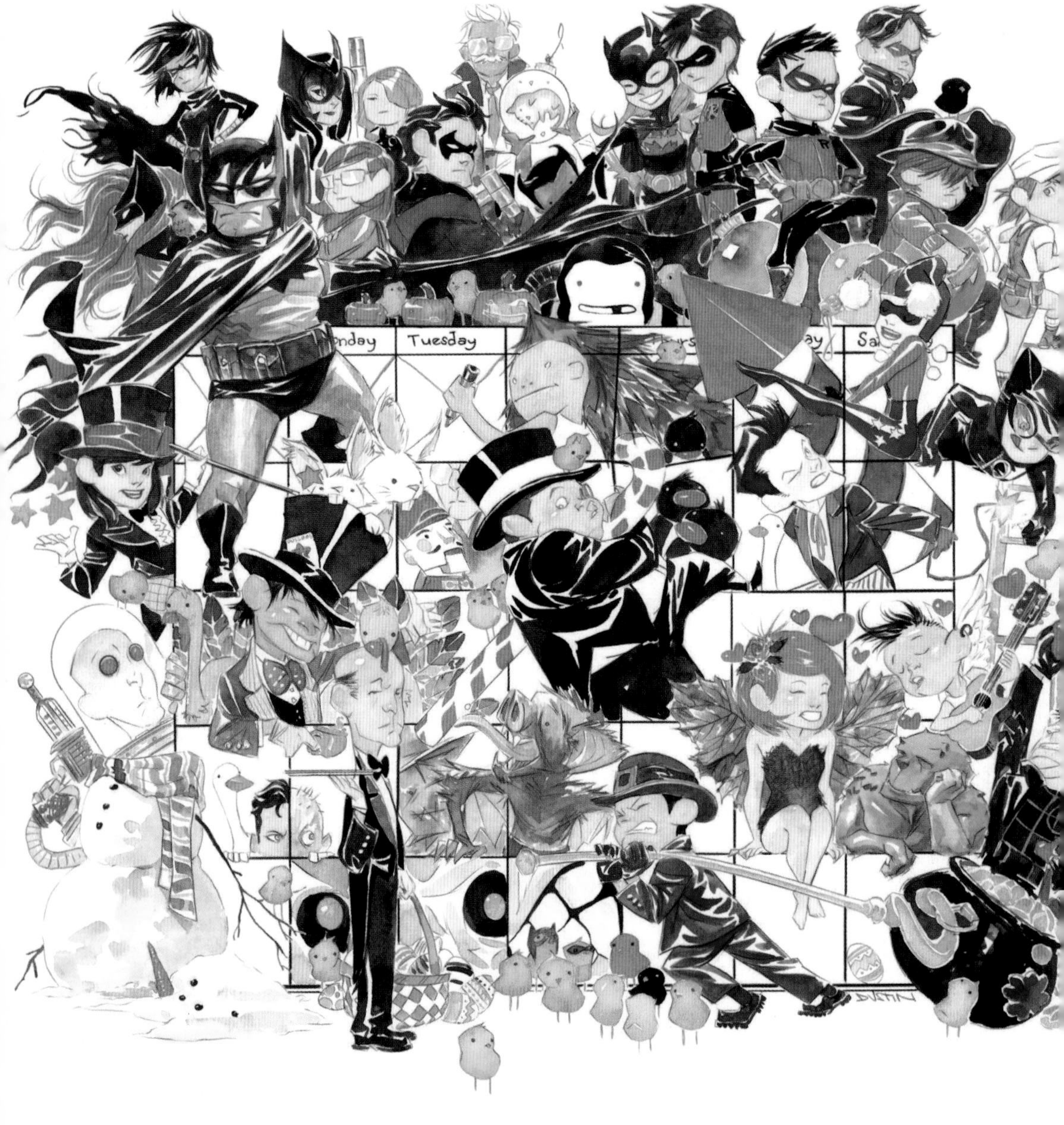
Tuesday

READ THEM ALL!

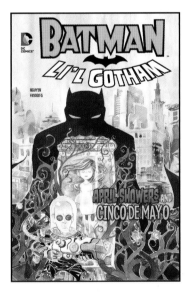

BATMAN™
LI'L GOTHAM